SPECIAL DELIVERY

A WRECKED HOLIDAY NOVEL

JODI PAYNE
BA TORTUGA

Special Delivery, A Wrecked Holiday Novel

Edited by Flat Earth Editing
https://www.flatearthediting.com/

Cover illustration by AJ Corza
http://www.seeingstatic.com/
Cover content is for illustrative purposes only and any person depicted on the cover is a model.

ISBN: 978-1-951011-37-6

Electronic edition published by Tygerseye Publishing, LLC, November 2020
Printed in the USA

1

"Thank you, ma'am. Yes, ma'am. No, sir, I'm retired. Nice to meet you, sir. Hey, kiddo, I like your hat."

Skyler had spent ten days doing publicity to support his annual Vermont invitational bull riding event that happened every spring. It was a big hit with the locals, and it drew folks from all over the country too, which made him popular in Burlington. He'd been shaking hands and signing shit like hats and programs, nodding, making goofy faces at babies, and pretending he was jealous that all the young guys were still riding.

Thank goodness for Danny, last spring's champ, and one of those younger riders. Danny was great at pulling people in, had three times his energy, and was eager to please.

With Danny's help, he'd secured sponsors and spread around a lot of good energy. But now he was sore, tired, and grumpy and ready to get home to his man and his critters. Flying, even in first class, was less than fun, and he had a husband waiting for him.

He finished his tomato juice and watched the orange and yellow trees. Pretty pretty.

The seat next to him was empty, which he appreciated, and he just wanted to rest until they landed. He knew Beckett was ready for him to get home too. They had to start doing the dance of his next exhibition.

This one would be number three, for chrissake. Number three in the spring, and Lord willing and the creek didn't rise, there'd be three of them too.

Lord help him. Miss Angie had caught pregnant straightaway; one time with the turkey baster, and she was ready to go. Beckett had done good homework. Whatever service he'd found hooked them right up—he'd just made a donation in a cup, and now their little one was cooking. They would be busy as all get out come the event.

"Sir, can you put your seat back up, please?" The stewardess was a pretty girl, all big black eyes and warm smile.

"Surely." He put the deal up, and then they were landing in short order. Lord have mercy, he was ready for this. As soon as they hit the ground, he turned his phone on.

It led to a bunch of texts.

Miss you.

Did you make your flight?

Are you home yet? I want to get my arms around you. That one was followed by a string of eggplants.

Please. Home btw. Yay.

Hey, husband. Where are you?

Pulling up to the gate. Be heading your way soon. Sky leaned a little hard on his cane when he stood, but he got his bag down without toppling over, or losing his hat, which was a win.

Beck caught sight of him before he made it off the escalator, and hurried his way. "Oh, my God! It's Skyler Paulson! Can I get an autograph?"

"You got a buck?" He winked at Beck, one arm sliding around his lover's back as he stepped off. It still felt bold as all get out to touch in public.

"I'm fresh out of bucks." Beck caught him up, taking some of his weight off his hip and hugged him tight. "You good? Welcome home."

"Thanks. Glad to be here." They headed for baggage claim to wait. "How's your week been?"

"Busy. I hated not coming with you, but...you know."

"Yeah, I know. Important man."

Beck let him lean a little bit more, handing off his phone. "Hey, did you see this yet? Angelica sent it a couple of hours ago. She had some weird cramping, and they sent her for an ultrasound." Beckett's hand tucked tighter around his waist. "She's fine. The baby is fine. She had...Braxton Hicks...or something. Fakey contractions. No big deal. But isn't our little Sky-ling perfect? The baby looks more like a baby and less like a blob this time."

His husband sounded so damn proud.

"Is she okay? Does she need anything?" Sky's heart raced at the thought of anything happening to either Angie or their wee one.

"She said she's fine. She was a little worried, but she's not anymore. I have a brief to get out, but maybe you could stop by with some of that ice cream she likes tomorrow and check in on her?"

"Sure." God, no. He wanted to sleep. Still, no rest for the wicked.

Beck grinned at him, eyes twinkling. "And so it begins, huh? Pretty soon I'll be on paternity leave."

"You'll be a man of leisure," he teased back. He'd never even heard of paternity leave, but it worked for them, yessir.

"Leisurely not sleeping, you mean?" Beck kept both

hands on the wheel but cut his eyes over to Sky. "I think it's time to put the nursery together. Order some furniture and all that. Paint. Pick some names."

"Okay. I'm good at putting shit together." He liked the whole idea of painting that little room, making it all fun and somewhere a baby belonged.

"So for boys I'm thinking Ozzy, or Axl...or maybe Mick," Beck grinned over at him. "Jimi? Elvis?"

"I will hurt you. No weird-assed names for my baby. Tanner, Dalton, Sterling, Stetson?"

"Stetson? Reel it in, cowboy." Beck laughed. "I like Dalton, though."

"Cheyenne if she's a girl?" He liked Cheyenne. "Or Dallas. Denver is unisex..."

Beck raised an eyebrow. "What's with the map names? You're not even from any of those places."

"What are your ideas, then? Lita? Madonna? Scary?"

"Ooh, Madonna." For a horrifying second, he thought maybe Beck was serious. "Scarlett. Violet. Hazel...or if you're not into colors maybe ice cream flavors. Vanilla, Raspberry..." Beckett was having way too much fun.

"Uh-huh. Brittany? Oakley? Shenandoah?"

"Shenandoah is kind of a mouthful, huh?" Beck snorted. "I'll play along. Charlotte? Elizabeth? Sierra?"

"I like Elizabeth and Sierra both." Actually, he thought they were beautiful. "Sierra Elizabeth. I like that."

"Oh. Sierra Elizabeth Paulson-Adler. That's nice." Beck reached over and squeezed his hand.

"It is!" Oh, one down, one to go. "Dalton MacKenzie after Mackey?"

Beck nodded. "Yes. After Mackey. Perfect."

"Wow." He looked over at his Beck. "That was easy. I missed you all week, bad."

Beck nodded as he pulled into the driveway. "Yeah. I was waiting on that until we got home." Even in the dark, he could see all the bushes in front had been trimmed and the garden beds were mulched for winter. Someone had been keeping himself busy this week. "And now we're home, so..." Beck parked the Jeep and shut it off, then pulled him closer by his shirt and kissed him hard.

The world stopped for a second, and his eyes rolled back in his head. Oh, thank fuck, that was perfect. He reached up and cupped Beckett's jaw, giving in to the pressure of those hungry lips.

Beckett kissed him until he could only gulp air, before letting him go. "Okay. You're home." Beck took a deep, heavy breath, jumped out of the Jeep, and came around to his side. "Now I can breathe. It's hard without you here."

"I'm home. I'm tired, but so fucking happy." Oh, the dog was losing his mind. Sky could hear him. He thought maybe he heard Walter too, meowing under the barking and howling.

"I'm not the only one who missed you. Bruiser's had his nose to that window for days, and Walter's been sulking." Beck scooped Sky right out of his seat and into his arms. "Hey, you."

"Hey, lover. Tell me I don't have to leave again forever." He rubbed their noses together, laughing at his weird codependence. Still, since they'd decided to have a baby, he found himself ready to nail his shoes to the floor.

"Never, ever." That was a lie and they both knew it, but it felt good to believe it right now. Beck carried him to the front door and set him down. "I'll get your suitcase. Don't let the furballs knock you over."

He braced himself and opened the door, Bruiser hitting

him like a ton of bricks. "Oh, my puppy. Has Walter been mean to you, you giant beast?"

Bruiser howled and moaned, telling him all about it, and all the while Walter was staring at him, tail twitching. *Uh-oh.*

"Bruiser! Down, boy. Inside, go on." Beck stepped around him and shooed the dog inside, then dropped his suitcase in the foyer. "Hey, Walt. Look who's home." Beck ran a hand over Walter's back and up the length of the cat's furry tail. "You want a beer? Should I order pizza?"

"Yes, and God, yes." He toed his boots off, putting them beside the door. "I brought you a present from Vegas."

"A present?" Beck pulled out his phone and Sky knew the pizza would be on its way shortly. His husband loved the whole ordering by app thing. "You mean other than the gift of finally having you here where I can touch you?"

"Yep, although that's pretty cool." He dug out the two bags. The first was a crazy mobile from one of the Cirque stores for the baby—the whole thing made from goofy little polka-dotted monsters. The second was another Venetian mask for the dining room. He'd been buying them for Beck for ages.

Beck's eyes lit up as he turned the mask over in his hands. "Oh, look at this one! A devil. Those horns...I love it, Sky." Beck kissed him and ducked into the dining room. "Where should we put it? I'll hang it tomorrow."

"Yeah? I'm glad you like it. I thought it went well with the winged one from last year."

"Yes. That's where we'll put it." Beck held it up on the wall near the winged mask. "Here."

Walter howled at them from the doorway like he was possessed.

"Uh-oh."

"Do you not want it there, Walt?" He needed the kitty treats. Stat.

Walter glowered at him, still as stone except for a jerky twitch of his tail.

"There's a can of tuna on the counter," Beck whispered, angling his head toward the kitchen.

"You are a gentleman and a scholar." He went and popped the can open. "Come here, sexy one."

Walter hesitated, but only for a second before waltzing into the kitchen with his head held high and his tail flagging. Bruiser followed, but Sky knew all he wanted was kisses. Walter required bribery.

He hand-fed his best bud with tuna, whispering to him about how he'd missed him most of all. Christ, he was owned.

Walter purred and devoured the offering, stopping every so often to trill at him and rub against his fingers. Beck distracted Bruiser with love and a chew toy, keeping the big fluff-ball out of their way.

"Walter won't admit it, but while you were gone...he slept with the dog again." Beck whispered the last bit. "On your side of the bed. Just like last time."

"Oh, he's my good buddy, you know. I don't know what I'd do without him." Walter had been there from the time he'd separated off from Beck, hopping right into his truck like he belonged there.

"Come get off that hip." Beck waited for him to wash the tuna off his fingers, handed him a beer, and led him to the sofa. "Now that all the animals have said hello, you think we can make out until the pizza gets here?"

Someone had missed him bad. "This is a marvelous fucking idea."

He took a drag of his beer, then pulled Beckett in for a hard kiss.

Beckett set his beer down with a loud thud on the table and held him with both hands. One of them caught him by the nape and the other gripped his shoulder as if making sure he were real. His husband's kiss was reassuring, but he could feel the rough need around the edges, the heat barely under control. He smiled against Beckett's lips, and found the heavy, denim-covered cock, rubbing nice and hard.

Damn, it was good to be wanted, to be desired. Craved, even.

"Sky." Beck had never been shy about what he wanted. Beck groaned and shifted, spreading to give Sky more access. Sky nodded, working open Beck's fly so he could fish out that sweet cock.

"I've been thinking about you all day." Beck dropped a hand low, trying to reach his fly but couldn't quite, so those hot fingers teased along his waistband instead.

"All day?" He stroked, base to tip, fingertip working the head. "I couldn't wait to get back to you."

Beck nodded, eyes starting to glaze over. "All week. But today, once I knew you were on that plane..." Beck pulled him into another kiss and rocked up into his fingers.

Someone wasn't going to have to sleep alone tonight, and he was getting laid too.

He dove into the kiss, humming into Beckett's mouth.

Beck shifted again stretching out and pulling Sky down on top of him, panting softly. Both hands worked his fly open. They'd never quite outgrown the appeal of rubbing off together. "This okay...on the hip?"

"Uh-huh. 'S okay. Want you." He got them lined up, just right. "Good?"

"So good." Beck's hands landed on his ass as he bucked up off the couch. "You...missed me, huh?"

"Every friggin' second." That was clear, right? "Every breath."

"Yeah." Beck nodded, breathing hard and hauling on his ass. The couch was creaking ominously, which would have been funny if they hadn't been so fucking focused.

They didn't have time to linger, either. That pizza was coming, and they didn't need to answer the door covered in spunk.

Beck shoved one hand between them and tightened it around both of their cocks, sweetening the friction. "Ready, baby?" Beck squeezed, giving him something to work against.

"Fuck!" He arched hard, driving them harder, pre-come slicking the way. "Beck. Beck, right there."

"Good, yeah? I've got you." Beck looked up at him, deep brown eyes holding his. "Close."

"Yes. Love you." More than anything on earth. He dove back into the kiss, both of them working together to get off.

"Mm. Mmm!" Most of Beck's shout was muffled by his lips, and Beck broke the kiss long enough to get a breath as wet heat spread between them. He followed right behind, only needing a stroke or two more.

He blinked at his lover, swaying a little, heart pounding hard. "Wow."

Beck chuckled and gave him a drunk-looking smile. "Always wow with you."

"No shit on that." He nibbled Beckett's bottom lip, as lazy as he could be.

"Love you, Stud." Beck kissed him, then rolled him suddenly, dropping him gently on the couch. "Let me clean up for the pizza guy. You relax." Beck had his shirt off before he'd even left the room.

Damn, he loved how Beck moved, like it was still easy. He envied that a little, but he liked watching it more. It was good to be home.

2

Beckett was tired in the best possible way. He'd kept his husband up late and woken him up early, and he wasn't sorry. Not one bit. Sky was out cold in bed when he left for work this morning and that was exactly how he wanted it. Sky needed two things when he got back from these publicity trips—him and lots of sleep.

Beck just needed Sky; he could manage fine without the sleep.

He hated that Sky had to travel alone sometimes, but it couldn't be helped. Beckett took off a big chunk of time in May to make sure he was available to help with Sky's namesake exhibition, and he couldn't do it again in the fall. The law firm had his name on it, and he had to be around to run it.

Besides, he wasn't useful shaking hands in Vegas. That was a picture-taking, media thing. He did his best work privately, chatting up sponsors and the social media people at the event itself. The VIP bar was essentially his office that week, and he knew how to work that crowd.

There was no crowd right now, though. Just the brief he'd been working to finish all morning. Because it had been on his mind, he'd also spent some time making a list for the nursery and thought about his paternity leave to discuss with Heath. Now that Sky was home, it was all about the baby coming in a short few months.

Their little baby Skyler. He couldn't wait to see Sky's eyes staring up at him from a tiny little baby face. He thought he understood boys better, but boy or girl, it really didn't matter to him, and he liked not knowing. Angelica, their surrogate, was due in late January, so the baby would be like a belated Christmas present.

He finished the last sentence on his brief, saved it, and emailed it to Jill to get her comments on it before he sent it to the client in the morning. Jill was brilliant. Heath had suggested they bring her on as a third partner in January, and he wasn't opposed except that it would mean finding another associate who could take her place, and those would be some big shoes to fill.

Heath was right, though. If they did decide to open up the partnership to a third attorney, she was ready. And if they didn't, they could lose her talent to someone else, and that would be a huge mistake.

He leaned back in his chair and checked his texts, finding the "good morning" one Sky had sent not too long ago.

You slept in. Good for you, he replied. *I'm going to try to head home early. Need me to pick anything up?* Sky was perfectly capable of getting in his own truck and running errands, but he still wanted to offer.

Nope. Love u. Gonna ice cream Angie, get steaks for 2nite. Feeling like we need the hottub after.

He heard that. That was code for Sky was hurting, and

the hot tub was one of the best spots to snuggle and help his husband relax and feel better. Hopefully it wouldn't take Sky a week or so to recover. Beckett felt a little badly about giving his husband a workout last night when he knew that hip was sore, but he hadn't heard Sky complaining. They'd needed each other.

Looking forward to that. I'll grab some wine. I want to hear all about your week.

Ditto. You want to meet for lunch? It did feel good, knowing that Sky missed him too, that his husband was craving him.

"Heath?" He hopped up out of his desk chair and ducked his head into his partner's office. "I was thinking about leaving early and meeting Sky for a late lunch. Would—"

"Give him my best. Tell him I saw one of his Facebook ads last night."

"Yeah? Cool. I'll let him know. You sure you don't mind?"

Heath rolled his eyes. "Really?"

Beckett laughed. "Okay, okay. Thanks. I'll be reachable if you need me."

"Not going to need you." Heath waved him off and went back to whatever he'd been typing.

Okay, then.

When and where? It's already late...maybe a beer at the P&B? The Vermont Pub and Brewery was a fixture in Burlington.

Absolutely. We can shop after & go see Angie and the baby together. See you there. <3

Beck sent some x's and o's. He was the luckiest man ever, and he was happy to take every opportunity to make sure Sky knew he thought so.

The P&B was walking distance for him, so he waited a

half an hour or so for Sky to get there and walked over, grabbing a seat at the bar. Sky might be more comfortable at a table, but sitting alone at a table always felt so weird.

He heard the warm greetings before he saw Sky, the happy laughter and hellos all around making him proud of his cowboy.

It was like Doc had once told him; Sky had never met a stranger. He loved how at home Sky was here now, making friends everywhere he went. Between his local practice and Sky's invitational, they'd become fixtures in Burlington. He waved so Sky would see him at the bar, but not to rush him.

Sky wandered over, the limp sort of pronounced today, and he got a warm smile, those pretty eyes taking him in. "Hello, gorgeous. How's your day going?"

"Good. Better now." Beck took Sky's hand and kissed it. "Did you have a nice drive? It's getting pretty out there." The leaves were just starting to turn. Another two weeks and the mountains would look like a painting.

"I did. When I left, Bruiser and Walter were sleeping together on the sofa." Sky pulled out his phone, showing off a photo.

Okay, that was adorable. A couple of Christmases ago, when he'd brought Bruiser home, it was partly because Sky was sure Walter needed a fluffy friend to keep him warm. At long last, it looked like maybe Sky was right. "Well, it only took nearly three years. Look at them." He slid off his bar stool. "Do you want a table?"

"I do." Sky took his hand and led him to one by the window. "A table, a beer, something crunchy coming—life is good."

"Crunchy?" He held Sky's chair for him. "What are you ordering?"

"Hmm...fried cheese? Fried things? I'm a fan of crunchy, salty goodness."

"Fried cheese. I'm so in." All he had to do was look up, and a server made his way over. "Hey, Rick." Rick had been there as long as he could remember.

"Hey, guys. What can I get you?"

He gestured to Sky. "He has ideas."

"Crunchy salty things. Something with cheese would be good. Anything that you can dip in ranch."

Rick laughed. "I think I can work with that. Beer?"

Beck nodded. "The usual."

"You got it. I'll be back, guys."

Beck smiled at Sky after Rick left. "So now that Walter has accepted Bruiser, how do you think he'll do with the baby?"

"He'll love her. Bruiser is going to think she's the best playmate ever."

"Her?"

Sky grinned. "Yep. I dreamed about her this morning."

Wow. "Really? Was she amazing? Did she have your gorgeous eyes and dark hair?" He couldn't wait to meet the baby—even a dream version was exciting.

"She was perfect and ours, and we brought her home." Sky beamed at him. "I'm excited to meet her, honey."

"Me too. I made lists today. I started looking at cribs." But he wanted to give his attention to his husband right now. "We're supposed to be talking about you. I'm sorry. How did you feel about the week?"

"It was good. Tiring—damn tiring—but I made the sponsors happy. I pulled some rope, went to a couple of after-parties." Sky shrugged and grinned at him. "Mostly I listened to the young kids and wondered if we were going to have a baby that got into rodeoing."

"Oh." That thought hadn't even occurred to him. He knew Sky wasn't going to like his initial reaction, so he didn't offer it. "Is that something you want?"

Sky stared at him like he'd grown another head. "Lord, no. Rodeoing is a hard fucking life with a short run and tons of scars and broken bones."

He let out the breath he'd been holding in a rush. "Oh. Good. I mean...I'd worry all the damn time." *Thank fuck.* He'd have compromised if it came to that, and who knew what having a former bull rider celebrity for a father would eventually mean, but he really didn't want to put his kid on a bull.

"Shit, baby, I rode bulls so there was enough money to send this kid to college. Ain't you ever heard 'Mammas Don't Let Your Babies Grow Up to Be Cowboys'?"

He laughed. "Yes. I have. Even we Yankees know Waylon and Willie." Although the Chipmunks version was his favorite. "You scared me for a second."

"Don't you worry, baby." Sky patted his hand. "She'll be a professor or a doctor or an interior designer. Something fancy."

Something safe. "Works for me. So your sponsors were happy? That's great. Danny's okay? He had a good summer, huh?" He should pay better attention to the rankings; he wasn't even sure who besides Danny was riding well this year.

"He's good. His little one is good. Everyone seems very young, you know? Or maybe I feel older. I'm not sure the fans are going to remember me much longer."

"They're young. But we're not old, Sky. We had this same conversation after the invitational in the spring, remember? You'll feel better once you're rested." Sky was sore and probably having some post-event letdown. Maybe Beckett should find a way to go next year, help keep his husband from working too hard. Keep his spirits up. "Hip hurts today, huh?"

"It's tender." Ah, tender. Cowboy-speak for it hurting bad enough that Sky would take a pain pill at some point today.

"Beer, gentlemen." Rick set down two tall drafts on the table.

"This'll help. Thanks, Rick." Beck picked up his glass, grinning. "To the hottest husband I've ever had."

"I'm the only husband you've ever had." Sky beamed at him, clinking their glasses together. "And I intend to let you keep me."

Beck nodded and winked. "As if I'd let you go." He took a sip of his beer, the cold and bitter bubbles exactly what he wanted. "Angelica said she'd help us pick out all the baby stuff. Apparently we need more than a crib and some diapers. Who knew?"

"I've been to the Walmart and seen the baby section. They need a metric fuckton of shit."

"I don't want a metric fuckton of shit, and Walmart always gives me a headache." Beck sighed. "The one in Williston? Is there where we need to go?"

Sky's eyes were dancing, evil bastard. "We can order baby fucktons from Amazon. Or go to Target. You like Target. I've seen the credit card statements."

"Target's closer, and it's the only place I can find my— shut up." Okay, he did have a bit of a Target habit. He narrowed his eyes at Sky. "I like Amazon just fine. I can compost the cardboard."

"You don't want to stroke the Target-y baby clothes? The teeny-tiny socks?"

He did. He totally did. "I hate you." He laughed and leaned back in his seat.

Skyler gave him a shit-eating grin, so perfectly happy. "So, food, Target, then the grocery, Angie, home, hot tub?"

"Steaks. Then hot tub. Then blowjobs...or did that go without saying?" He knew damn well that Sky would be toast after the hot tub, and he'd get to fall asleep with a warm, doped up, cowboy. But it was fun to play anyway. "Let's save Target for another day after we've talked to Angelica. More hot tub time." And less time Sky had to be on that hip.

"Yeah? I'll take you tomorrow, if you want." Sky nodded, boot toe nudging his ankle. "More hot tub time sounds like heaven."

He smiled and turned his ankle to bump that boot right back. "Tomorrow works." The only plan he had for tomorrow was to spend his time with Sky.

Rick set down a plate of fried things, grinning. "Fried mozz, popcorn chicken, fried jalapeno slices, fried mac and cheese...ranch dip."

"You are a gentleman among men." Sky hooted, the rednecky sound filling the air and making everyone chuckle.

Rick laughed and gave Sky a clap on the shoulder. "That reaction made the way the chef looked at me worth it. Call me if you guys need anything else."

"Thanks, Rick! Look at this." He reached for a slice of fried jalapeno first.

"*Uhn.* Spicy goodness. Gimme." Sky opened his lips, begging.

He laughed as he reached out and popped the crunchy bite into Sky's mouth.

Sky hummed and chewed, making the best little sex noises.

"You know what we should do? We should take a trip. Maybe around Thanksgiving or something, get away before the baby comes and we can't for a while. Europe maybe. Or Hawaii. Someplace we haven't been yet."

"Yeah? I've been to Hawaii. How about Australia? I want to go there and see kangaroos."

"God, I'd love to, but I don't think I can get that much time off right before paternity leave...I was thinking like a five-day trip, you know? So Heath would only have to cover a couple of days." Heath had been a good sport, but Australia would probably be pushing it.

"Okay. We'll go with the baby when she's old enough. How about Jackson Hole? We can pretend to be fancy."

"Ooh. We could. I could wear the nice felt hat you bought me. I rock that thing." They could ski a little or pretend to and hang out in the saunas.

"Good deal. I'll do some research for us and let you know what all I find." Sky was a master at arranging travel, from flights to cars to hotels, and even better, he loved it.

"My personal travel agent. God, these popcorn chicken things are so good." Fried food...he was going to have to add a couple of miles to his runs this week, but it would be so worth it.

"Uh-huh. Fried food is proof that God is real, and He loves us to crunch." Sky dipped in the ranch. "Ranch is more Jesus-y. Smoother, creamy, less vengeful."

"Weirdo." He didn't need proof. All the proof he needed was sitting right in front of him, munching happily. He'd come too close to losing Sky not to understand a gift when he saw one. "Have you ever had fried pickles? Now those are a spiritual experience."

"Feed me, baby."

There was nothing—nothing—like a happy, healthy cowboy, staring at him over a table, wanting a bite.

Beckett thought he was the luckiest son of a bitch on earth.

3

"Walter, if you walk in that paint, I will let Beck serve you as pâté to the Chamber of Commerce. Mint green is not your color." To be honest, Sky wasn't sure mint green was anyone's color. Was this a good thing? For their baby to wake up to faded Kermit for a chunk of their life?

He had liked the SpongeBob yellow a lot, but Beck had been downright stubborn on that front.

Walter sat right where he was and started giving himself a bath, as if to say he had better things to do than mess with the stupid mint-green paint. At least Walter was cooperating. Bruiser was in his crate. He was not to be trusted.

Paint wasn't permanent, right? He could change it any time. The old cream color that was in here before had to go, in any case.

"Maybe we could do a wall in peach, one in baby blue, one in pink, and one in mint green. That would be fun. I bet Beck wouldn't even notice, right Walter?" He dipped the paintbrush in and gave the paint a try.

Nope. Still didn't love it.

He knew that green was the universal gender-neutral thing, but he had feelings. He'd do one wall so they could look at it objectively, but he was going to have to discuss it with Beck.

"Hey, Stud. I found the painter's...tape. Oh." Beck stopped in the doorway to the nursery and frowned. "That's...hm."

"Ugly. Butt ugly is the term you're searching for, baby." He wanted something less ice cream and more joyous.

"Butt fucking ugly. Fugly. That's awful, put that away." Beck shook his head. "My bad. I take full responsibility."

"Oh, good. Let's pick something less moldy-looking." Sky beamed, feeling utterly vindicated. "Blue? Purple? Peach? Sun colored? Ooh...UT orange?" They could decorate in longhorns.

"Ah, there it is. I've been waiting for the Texan to step in here. You want big horns up over the crib, too?" The look on Beck's face was inscrutable. He wasn't sure whether his husband was joking.

"We could paint them on the crib. I think real ones might be a little pokey for the baby." Still, maybe stuffed ones...

"Or maybe one of your sponsors could make her a mobile out of them." Beck grinned, but then his phone rang, and he pulled it out of his pocket. "You really want orange? Oh, it's Heath. On a Saturday." Beck frowned and answered the call. "Hey, Heath, what's up? What?"

That was followed by the heaviest silence he'd felt in a long while. Beck leaned against an unpainted wall, listening intently. He glanced up only once with sad brown eyes and shook his head. When Beck finally spoke again, his voice was rough.

Something was wrong. Something terrible had happened.

"Okay. Yeah." Beck cleared his throat. "I have no idea if he...yeah. I—we'll figure it out. Do we need to come get them or...okay. Talk soon."

Beck ended the call.

"Baby? What's wrong?" He didn't tease, didn't bullshit. Whatever it was, they'd reckon it. "Is Heath okay?"

Beck looked at him. "It's Connor. A truck lost control on I-89 and..." Beck clenched his jaw and shook his head.

"You mean Connor White? Jesus, baby, he called not—" His eyes went wide. "He asked you to go with him."

Connor had wanted to do...something. Hell, Sky didn't even remember, but Beck had said no, that they were painting the baby's room.

It could have been his Beckett.

"He was on his way back from White River Junction." Beckett was white as a sheet. "I have to go get the kids."

"Okay, let's go." He wasn't sure where the kids were or why they were getting them, but if they needed to fetch them, get them they would. "Walter. Get out of here. I'll shut the paint in."

"Thank God they weren't in the car." Beck walked out of the room and down the stairs like a robot. "They're so little. And Laurie just...not even a year ago."

He remembered that, when Connor and the kids had lost Laurie to cancer. The whole community came out. She'd been way too young.

"Who's got the kids?" He wasn't sure exactly why they were going to get them still, but he could drive. "Laurie's folks?"

He knew Connor'd lost his mom to cancer before he'd even married Laurie.

"They're with the sitter at the house, and the police are there waiting for us. The kids don't have grandparents. They —*shit*." Beck turned to him and took his hands, squeezing them tight. "Sky. They don't have anybody. They just have me. Well, us. After Laurie died, Connor asked if he could name me guardian in his will, and of course I said yes, but I never imagined...Sky, those little ones are going to be ours now."

Sky blinked. "Say what?"

At some point he smelled too much of that no-fumes paint—and he'd told Beck that it was a lie, that it was just no-stink paint and it would kill brain cells, and Beck didn't believe him—and he was having a weird-assed, mint-green fucking dream.

Because they had a baby coming in twelve-ish weeks.

Their baby.

"Yeah. Okay." Beck took a deep breath and puffed it out, and that sad look in his eyes disappeared. "We just have to step up for a minute, Stud. We can think about all of this later." Beck grabbed his keys.

"I'm driving, and I'm going to step up, but I think you got some explaining to do." Starting with how it was okay to agree to take two kids without saying anything to your husband, immediately followed up by how many more of Beck's friends' kids might end up being theirs, because he was going to have to start building on.

"I know, I know." Beck put his keys back and handed him his jacket. "It's a million years too late for an apology, though, so I'm not sure what to say."

Sky didn't know what to say either, so he went with his granddaddy's favorite adage— "Taste your words before you spit them out, boy, just in case you have to eat them later."

He'd keep his mouth shut, and once Beckett figured out

whatever lawyer-y way to say, "I suck" and "I'm sorry," he'd decide whether to snarl.

Beckett was silent for most of the drive. Sky sure didn't have anything to say, so the drive was quiet. As they got closer to Connor's house, Beck finally looked at him again. "I blew it. Connor was so alone at the time, and I was trying to make him feel better, you know? And...this was obviously a much bigger deal than I thought it was at the time, and I should have told you—no, I should have *asked* you how you felt about it before I told him he could put me in his will. I'm sorry, Sky." Beck let out a sigh and looked down at his hands. "I'm really sorry."

"Yeah." Sky wasn't sure what to do, except drive. Well, okay, he did know one thing. "We'll figure it, baby. One way or the other."

"I can't believe this. I can't believe I just talked to him a few hours ago and now...he was picking up a dollhouse for Charlotte and wanted company. I can't believe it." Beck took another deep breath and pressed the heels of his hands to his eyes. "Jesus, I can't do that right now, can I?"

"Buck up, cowboy. Unless I misunderstand, we ain't got a whole lot of choices." He sighed softly and shook his head. "One thing at a time. We fetch the babies, we get them to the house and fed and shit. You and me talk about our options."

He needed to understand exactly what the deal was, so he could figure out...everything.

"They really are babies, Sky. Charlotte is three and Noah is not even two yet." Beck pointed. "That's his driveway."

"Okay. You want me to deal with this, so you don't have to go in?" Babies were just like any little critter—they required calm.

"No. I've got this. I probably have to deal with the police

anyway." Beck shook his hands out and puffed out a breath as Sky parked. "Okay. I'm good."

"All right. Let's go in. You remember to be calm, okay? The sitter is probably losing her mind, and you can't load up on a bull if you're mind ain't in the middle."

Beck turned suddenly and reached for him, pulling him into a hard kiss. "Thank you. I love you." Beck gave him a quick nod and hopped out of the truck.

"That I know, you giant, beautiful bastard." He chuckled and got out of the truck, feeling like he was fixin' to wander into a war.

Beck took his hand as they walked up to the house and a uniformed officer opened the door before they got there.

"Can I help you?"

"Beckett Adler. This is my husband, Skyler."

"Good to meet you. Come on in."

Beck was dragged off into a discussion with the cop, leaving him and the babysitter staring at each other in the kitchen. She was probably twenty or so, a college kid or something. She looked terrified and in way over her head.

"I packed bags for them and folded up the portable crib...that was Officer Jones's suggestion."

"Good deal. Did you watch them a lot, honey?"

"I was—yeah. Once a week or so."

Poor little girl. He felt for her, and he suddenly wanted to call the half a dozen buddies from the circuit with multiple babies and ask for help. That would be a plan for later. Right now he was going to pretend he was buying foals. "So, can you tell me what this old cowboy needs to know about them? The short version? I know you'll want to go home soon, but I need to know things like what all they eat, did Connor give you emergency numbers, what Miss Charlie sleeps with."

How the hell he was supposed to deal with this shit? Somehow he doubted this little gal had that—

"Cowboy Sky?" He heard Miss Charlie's voice, and he turned and smiled at her.

"Hey, girlfriend! I been missing your pretty face."

Fuck a doodle goddamn doo.

She went right to him and leaned on his leg. "Lacey, I'm hungry."

Lacey found a convincing smile and dug some Goldfish crackers out of a cabinet for her. "Take these with you." She set the rest of the bag down on the counter.

"Noah is sleeping," Charlotte told him, munching on crackers.

Lacey started wandering around the kitchen and packing up a grocery bag with food and snacks. "He has a little notebook for his sitters. I packed it too. Her favorite is her fuzzy duck, and she likes her books."

"You got those in a bag?"

She nodded, tears starting to fall, and Sky went to her. "You did good. Real good, girl. Let me pay you. Can—are you willing to sit sometimes? We got a baby due after the first of the year."

Her eyes went wide. "Oh, my gosh." She searched around for a pen and pulled a pad off the fridge. "I'm always looking for extra cash, I'm...between stuff right now. Here's my cell. Call any time, I have a car." She handed him the note. "Lacey Brown," it read, with her number underneath it. "I don't want money for today, though. Thank you."

"Are you sure? I know how it is." He winked over at her, his eyes taking in all the shit in this house. Were they fixin' to have to deal with this too? "I was a rodeo cowboy. I have been so far down, the ninety-nine-cent menu was my entire nutritional input. You aren't being disrespectful for getting paid for your work."

"I...yeah. Well, not for today." She shook her head. "Thank you, though." She gave him a half smile. "I thought you were *that* Sky. I love your event up here."

Beck and the officer joined them. "Do you know where an extra set of keys might be?"

"Oh. Yes. There's a ring..." Lacey searched her mind for a second, then opened the door to the basement. "Here it is. Everything is on here...the shed out back, the garage, the generator, all kinds of stuff."

The officer took the ring and handed it to Beckett. "I'm done here, I guess. I'll check in with you in a couple of days. My condolences."

"Thank you." Beck saw the officer to the door.

"He left the car seats. He always leaves the car seats in case of emergen—" Lacey started to sob, and Sky eased her toward the door.

"You come by and see the kids in a few days. I'll call you, okay?"

They didn't need hysteria yet. That would come tonight. Not yet, please, God.

"Okay. Thank you." She sniffled but let herself be led.

Beck picked up on what he was doing and walked Lacey right out to her car. He was back in two minutes and closed the front door quietly. "Hey, Charlie. You got some Goldfish, huh?"

She nodded and offered him one. "Lacey gave them to me."

"Oh, no thank you. I'm full." Beck looked at him. "We have a lot to talk about. Should I...I should get stuff."

"Lacey did some packing already. Fuzzy duck. Books." He sighed softly. A lot to talk about. *Shit.* "Hey, girlfriend, you and your brother want to come to our house and have a slumber party?"

"A slummer party?" Her eyes went wide.

"Yep. We can watch movies, eat popcorn, and sleep on the sofa. Walter and Bruiser would love to see you."

"Can Apple and Violet come?"

Please, God, if you love me, don't let those be mice. I hate mice.

He looked at Beckett with a smile that had to look as fake as it felt.

"Can we come back for Apple and Violet tomorrow? I'll bring something we can carry them in safely, okay?" Beck kissed her cheek. "Okay. I'll get the stuff Lacey packed, and put the car seats in your truck..."

"Is it cool, Miss Charlie? You want to come hang with me?" He held his arms open, and thank God, she came to him.

"We got to get the baby."

"We do. Let's get him; you can go potty and pick a toy out of your room to play with tonight while I change his butt. Or does he go to the bathroom by himself now?"

Charlie giggled at him. "You have to change his butt!"

That even got a little chuckle out of Beckett as he hauled the portable crib out the front door.

By the time Beck had the truck packed and the rest of the house locked up, Sky and Charlie had fed Apple and Violet—who turned out to be fish, hallelujah—and tucked Noah into his car seat.

"All right, Miss Charlie. Let's go see Bruiser and Walter. Chicken nuggets for supper cool with you?" He listened to her jabber as he loaded her in the truck and got in himself. Soon they were headed down the road, and his head was pounding, his hip was screaming, and he was trying his best not to think.

Thinking wasn't his damn strong suit.

"We can put the little fold-up crib in the nursery, and I think I have one of those Aerobed things in the basement for her." Beck was mostly quiet on the drive home, but every so often he'd say something like that. Beck was doing plenty of thinking for both of them.

"The nursery has had an open can of paint in it all day. We'll have a slumber party tonight." And talk. Hard.

"Sh—ure thing. Right." Beck rubbed his forehead with his fingers. "Dinner and then we can put on a movie for the slumber party." Beck's hand landed on his thigh, thumb rubbing over his denim in slow circles.

"We can. We'll wear our jammies."

"Mine are Moana!" Charlotte said, and he nodded to her in the rear view, even as Noah crowed, then started babbling.

"Mine are plaid," Beck told her. Sky didn't think he'd ever seen Beck in actual pajamas. "Red plaid. A little warm for this time of year but they'll work."

"You can be like Daddy and not wear a shirt. He's always hot."

"What are Noah's favorite pajamas?" Beck asked, covering well when his voice caught in his throat.

"Well, he has Superman ones, but he likes his yellow giraffe ones best."

"Excellent." Sky tried to think what he had in his travel shit. "Mine are Ninja Turtles."

"Turtle power!"

"That's right!" God, let him get them home.

"Turtle power?" Beck looked at him as he finally turned down their rural, bumpy road. "I guess I grew up under a rock. Oh. Home." Beck stretched and rolled his shoulders. "How do you want to handle dinner and stuff? You want to sit for a bit? I can bring everything in."

"I'm going to order supper. We're going to introduce the kids to Bruiser, and then we'll figure out what happens next." And he was going to have a shot, a pain pill, and a mostly silent freak-out when he put on his PJs.

"Okay." Beck nodded slowly, so on his wavelength. "Good plan."

He parked the car and Beck went to get Noah, which meant he didn't have to worry about carrying anybody. Instead, he let Charlie out of her car seat and went to deal with Bruiser.

"Hey there, big guy," Beck said to Noah softly. "You ready for a sleepover?" Noah squirmed and Beck let go and let him walk.

"Doggie!" Noah shouted, pointing at Bruiser in the window.

"Yes." And thank God they'd been spending time training and getting Bruiser around kids since they'd started planning this baby thing. "Bruiser, sit."

His good boy plopped his ass right down, wagging furiously.

The true test of Bruiser's patience, though, was when both kids mobbed him, hugging and kissing him and telling him he was a good boy. Bruiser couldn't have been happier. His tail kept wagging, and he bathed both babies' faces with his tongue. Noah squealed, and Charlie told him to shush, but Bruiser sat there on cloud nine, like the happiest pup on earth.

"Oh, good boy, Bruiser." Beck praised him and pet his head. "Good boy."

"Yes. He is." He searched for Walter, who was at the top

of the cat condo, glaring. "Y'all leave the kitty alone, okay? He's a little grumpy."

Charlie looked up at Walter. "What's her name?"

"His name is Walter. He just needs some time to figure you guys out, okay?"

Charlie waved but didn't get any closer. "Hi, Walter."

Walter's ears twitched and his tail went thump against the cat tree.

"I'm hungry." Charlie tugged on his jeans.

"Oh." Noah wandered off into the house and Beck followed. "I'm on it."

"I'll order supper. Would you like some more Goldfish while we wait?" They needed to get the baby gates out of the garage.

"Okay. I like Goldfishes. Your house is pretty."

"Thank you, honey. I'm so glad you think so. Noah? You want some Goldfishes?"

"Go-fishes!" Noah came running, Beck right behind him.

"You got them a second? I'll unpack the truck." Beck kissed his cheek. "Then I'm pouring a little something."

"Yeah." He scooped up the little one. "Go-fishes! Let's have some at the tab—" No. They were too short. "How about on a blanket on the couch?"

"Like a picnic." Charlie was all over that. Noah blew a raspberry in his ear.

"Like a picnic." Sky told himself that he was cool. Like chilly.

And if he didn't get a chance to gnaw on his husband's ear, life was fixin' to get plumb icy.

4

———

Beckett sat up very, very slowly, holding a sacked-out Noah against his chest. He gingerly dropped his legs over the side of the rollout couch and stood, tiptoeing to the little portable crib.

He glanced at Sky, who nodded silently for him to try to put the baby down.

Here goes nothing.

Beckett bent and lowered Noah into the crib, placing him gently on his tummy and covering him with the little blanket Lacey had put in with the baby's things. Noah wiggled and stuck his thumb in his mouth but stayed fast asleep.

He gave Sky a thumbs-up and went over to see if he could extract his husband from underneath Charlotte. Neither of them was at their best, but they needed to have a talk anyway, away from little ears. He was hoping they could do it with a snuggle and some whiskey. The latter was a sure bet, the snuggle...well, he'd have to take Sky's temperature on that one. Maybe after the whiskey.

She moved into the corner of the sofa with a grunt and a

sigh, and Sky covered her up, keeping her all settled in before they moved together to the kitchen.

Beck didn't ask, he just pulled out two glasses and poured out a couple of fingers of whiskey for each of them. "Have your pain meds kicked in?" Whiskey, pain meds... whatever. It wasn't like Sky made a habit of it. He dropped an ice cube in his drink and offered one to Sky.

"Thank you." Sky sighed and swirled the ice in the glass, lips tight.

He took a sip and leaned against the kitchen counter, watching Sky as the whiskey burned just right going down, waking him up and helping him focus. He knew two things: hard things needed to be said, and whatever else happened, at the end of the day he and Sky were going to be okay. "Say whatever you need to say, Sky. It doesn't have to be polite. Lay it on me."

"You can't just agree to do something huge, honey. Shit happens. I know it happens in my world a shit-ton more than yours, but...you got to let me in."

He nodded. "It didn't feel as huge when I agreed as it does right now, for sure. You're right. I should have asked you first." He swirled the ice cube around and took another sip; then he looked at Sky. "But that begs the question... would you have said no?"

"I doubt it." The speed of the answer proved that Sky had been thinking about that same thing. "I would have gambled that he would have gotten together with another lady, gotten remarried, changed his will. It would have been a reasonable thing to do for a friend."

"That's what I thought at the time. I didn't really internalize what he was asking me. I didn't actually think, 'What if?' " He shrugged. "I'm sorry."

"Me too. About Connor, more than anything. So, what

happens now? I mean, seriously, what are we supposed to do?"

He swallowed the knot that tried to ride in his throat at the mention of Connor's name. He'd deal with that. He'd take a walk or go chop some wood or something and think about Connor later. Tomorrow. He had shit to do right now.

"Okay." He downed the rest of his drink and set it on the counter. "Heath is reading the will, and he'll get back to us about the legal stuff, but Heath was officially named executor, so we don't have to do much of anything except take care of the kids. He'll deal with the estate and setting up trusts or whatever has to happen, and he said not to stress it, he'd walk us through everything."

He reached for Sky's hand. He needed a little...contact. He needed his husband. "So I guess we have to talk about how we're going to do this."

Mentally, he was already making a list. He'd go get the fireplace gate from Connor's tomorrow to babyproof their wood stove. Put up the gates in the garage. Load up Sky's truck with Charlotte's bed and Noah's changing table and...

He'd better get a pen.

"So...they're ours now? Just like that?" Sky looked a little green around the gills, but he didn't raise his voice.

"Barring one day in court when the judge will look at us and ask if we agree to take them on and care for them as our own...yes. They're ours now. We're all they have for family."

He knew how Sky felt. Even if they'd both agreed to this, even if Sky had been on board a year ago when Connor had asked him...they'd still be right here. Shocked. Off-balance. Trying not to fucking panic.

"Unless we decide to say no in court. A will isn't the law. We still have to agree."

"And then what? They go into the system, get split up?

Shit, I'm not that big of an asshole. I sure didn't expect to go from one on the way to two in the bush, though, and I'm just..." Sky swallowed and shook his head. "I'll run over there first thing in the morning and pick shit up, get more paint and all."

"Did you get Lacey's number? Maybe she can come stay with them for a bit and we can go together. You..." He almost said Sky shouldn't be carrying things up and down the stairs on his own with the bad hip, but that was all Sky needed to hear right now. "You and I will need to make some decisions together about what to bring over from the house. I know I want the wood stove gates. We'll need those."

"Yeah." Sky went to the junk drawer and pulled out a pad and a pen. "So, what else can you think of?"

"Charlotte's bed. Noah's crib. Medical files, but we might need to get those through Heath. Clothes, toys, we might as well grab all of that, right?"

Pictures. Family shit. Someone was eventually going to have to figure out what to save for the kids. Were they going to have a funeral? Would Connor even want one? *Jesus.* He didn't know if he could do that. But he didn't know if he had a choice.

Sky scribbled lists, four of them, each in its own quadrant. His weirdly organized cowboy.

"Hey, Sky? You want me to fly my mom up? She'd be here in a heartbeat. I know she would." He could bring them both up—Dad loved Vermont, loved the trees—but Dad had never understood bull riding or Sky really at all, and Sky didn't need more stress. Mom was good, though, she loved Sky.

"Where are we going to put her? At this point, we have an empty nursery and a guest room that's fixin' to get two little beds in it tomorrow, plus our office, which looks like a hoarder room. I'm going to make myself a man cave in the goddamn basement behind the dryer."

"Seems reasonable. You're basically a hobbit."

"I've heard that before. I'm way hotter." Sky bent back to his lists.

"Hottest thing in a cowboy hat." He moved in on Sky and tucked an arm around his waist, reading over Sky's shoulder. "So no Mom. And move the office to the basement? Or...we have the living room down here and the family room. We never use that living room." Only when his parents visited. Otherwise they spent all their time in the family room. It was warm, it had a TV, it was right off the kitchen.

"It's bigger than the office, and we could put a bassinet in." Sky sighed softly. "Okay. So, get the kids' stuff, move the office down, get a contractor in to redo the basement for a guest room. Buy more Goldfish crackers and a Walter-proof fish tank."

"Assuming there is such a thing as Walter-proof." He tightened the arm he already had around Sky, pulling Sky back against his chest. "I love you. I don't know how we're going to work all of this out yet, but we will. We can do this." He sighed, suddenly remembering what the cop had told him. "Oh. One more thing."

He felt Sky stiffen up in his arms. "One more thing?"

"Yeah. The kids don't know. I'm sure Noah is...but nobody told Charlotte anything."

"Of course they didn't." Sky nodded once. "I'll talk to her tomorrow before we bring her shit in."

Part of him wanted to say he'd do it, and part of him was ridiculously grateful that Sky offered first. To be honest, Sky had a way with words, he knew how to talk to people, and Beckett actually thought he'd do a better job. But that didn't make it a job anyone wanted to have. "Are you sure? I don't want to put that on you."

"Well, I do like to get my 'Gee, your daddy's dead' conversations done early in the day, so I can save my afternoon for moving furniture." Sky stood and shook his head. "Yeah. I'll do it. I'm just pissed at God right now."

He let Sky go, but reluctantly. "Well, until you're good with him again, you've got me." He understood. He wasn't even going to try to reconcile this with God yet. "Why don't you go sleep upstairs where you'll be comfortable. I can sleep down here on the roll-out with the kids." They'd bought a good mattress for their bed a couple of years ago when it became clear Sky was going to have hip issues on and off.

"It's—okay, look, you know what? No. No, this is not okay. None of this is okay. We are supposed to be celebrating and painting and looking forward to the birth of our baby. Not panicking and tap-fucking-dancing around each other trying to figure out what the hell we're supposed to do now! I am not in any motherfucking way okay. I am fucking pissed off." Sky could scream-whisper with the best of them.

That was okay to say? They were allowed to be pissed off? He didn't want to be an asshole, and it had nothing to do with Connor or those sweet kids sleeping in the family room, but this was kind of a disaster. They'd had plans. Good ones. Joyful ones. "This is pretty fucked up, huh?"

"You think?" Sky arched one eyebrow. "I won't hate those babies. I won't be evil. But I'm not happy. I wanted—shit, I wanted a lot of shit for the next few months I ain't gonna get."

"Hey." He caught Sky's arm and pulled him closer. "Let's not trash it all yet. We still have our baby coming. That's still amazing and wonderful. I can't quite see where we'll be in a month right now, but that doesn't mean we have to totally throw our hands up."

"Beck, I love you with all my heart, but if I want to privately lose my motherfucking mind for a few hours, I'm allowed." The words and the tone didn't match. Like at all.

"Yeah, you are allowed. And not only today. You can lose it on me any time. I just wanted you to know I'm going to help you put it back together. Fuck, Sky. I'm not there yet, but it's coming. I know it is. This makes no sense, it's not fair, it's not what anyone wanted." He had a date with that woodpile. Soon.

"No. No, but we're not spending the night apart, either. We can sleep on the sofa. We can bring Charlie up to our bed. I don't care, but dammit, I spent all the nights without you I intend to have."

Damn. Sky hit the nail on the head there, didn't he? "Whatever you want to do. I won't sleep really without you anyway." Especially not tonight. They'd had way too many close calls of their own. "I can carry her up, we can use the baby speaker thingy for Noah." *Jesus.* All these baby gadgets had names, didn't they? "Monitor. Baby monitor."

"We can take them both up, put his bed next to ours. It'll take us a few days to arrange...shit, everything. And you're back to work Monday, right?"

He shook his head. "No. No, I'll lose my fucking mind. I need a few days. Heath will understand." But he would be back at work eventually, and that would leave Sky single-parenting all day long. They were going to have to discuss his schedule. There had to be some options—he was his own goddamn boss, wasn't he? Not tonight, though.

"Okay, let's get you and Charlie up, and we'll make some space for Noah. First, though? I want a kiss."

"Yeah?" Sky came to him, holding his gaze. "I love you.

Even when shit sucks, I love you. I got zero idea how this is going to work, but at least...well, we wanted a family, I guess, and now we got a daughter and a son and another on the way—I'm about positive that is a lyric in a country song."

"That's my cowboy." Sky could be frustrated and mad for a minute, but fundamentally, his husband was an optimist. "I think maybe I love you even more when things suck because you're there to help me through it. And I bet that's a country song too." He pulled Sky in close and kissed him, pouring everything in his heart into it.

He was scared as hell, and he was going to have to mourn his friend, but Sky was here with him, solid as a rock, a cowboy, through and through.

Day by day. They'd get through tomorrow and see what happened next. He stepped back from Sky and smiled. "You ready?" He wasn't. Not at all. But it didn't feel like it mattered in that moment.

5

Sky let Beckett drive back to the house. He was exhausted down to the bone, between the stress and the anger and the long night of talking to God with an early morning of little ones.

He didn't understand what he was supposed to learn from this, but he had to have faith there was a reason to things, a bigger hand putting him here now.

His husband sipped coffee from a travel mug as they drove and didn't have much to say. He was totally in his head this morning, thinking hard. Sky wasn't worried; this was trademark Beckett—mind always looking forward, searching for options, trying to find solutions. It was exactly how his husband processed everything.

Still, just when he started to wonder if Beck was shutting him out, a hand settled on his thigh and he relaxed a little. They were so together in this.

"I wish we had a little trailer to move things. We might have to get one." A trailer for his pickup and an SUV for three car seats after the year changed. *God.*

"That, or a roof rack for all the car seats. We can line

them up." Beck shook his head. "Neither of us has a car that will fit three car seats. We better add that to your list."

"Yeah. Big safe car. Trailer. Everything else." He snorted at himself. "Lord. We still got to decide on colors for the nursery. You think we ought to paint the office something lighter?"

"Well, the room needs a coat of paint anyway, so why not? I actually think it will be a nice office. There's the fireplace, the windows, a nice view. We can get new furniture, set it up right instead of tossing it together like it is now. Even if we can't get to that right away, it can be in the plan. Silver lining, right?"

Beck turned down Connor's long, gravel driveway and frowned. "Is someone here? What's going on? Who is that?"

"Fuck if I know. My shotgun's under the seat. Hold up."

"You can take the cowboy out of Texas..." Beck put a hand on his shoulder. "Wait a second. I think that's Heath." Beck drove up slowly and parked behind another truck that was loaded up with... "And I think that's a crib. What the hell?"

Heath waved to them both, grinning. "Happy Sunday, gentlemen."

Beck went over and shook Heath's hand. "What are you doing?"

"Hey, Beck." That was Jake Keller climbing off the truck bed. And Paul Harding was carrying a duffel bag out of the house.

"Hi...guys." Beck looked a little stunned.

"Hey, y'all." Beck may not know what this was, but he sure did. This was good folks doing good deeds. "We appreciate the hand."

"Heath. You didn't have to—"

Heath was only a little bit younger than Beckett, but the

man's full beard, height, and broad shoulders made him seem older. "Beck, this is easy. You're doing the hard part. I'm the executor, so I'm just doing what I'm allowed to do. Provide for those kids. With a little help."

"You're a good man, buddy. Where are we? What all do we need to do still? That Lacey-gal has the kids."

"We dismantled the kids' room. All of that is going in the truck for you now. You guys should go in and figure what else you want. Honestly, everything is fair game because it will get sold if you don't take it."

Beck squinted at the house. "Okay."

"Nothing's getting sold for weeks, take what you need today, come back for what you want later."

"We need to get the fish and clean out the fridge and pantry. That part's important." Sky tried to remember what Beck had wanted. "And the fireplace screen deal."

"Yeah. We'll go have a look around."

"Go for it. You've got us all day."

Beck blinked. "All day?"

"Sure. We need to make sure those kids are comfortable, and you guys are on your feet. We have time."

"Wow." Beck took Sky's hand. "You ready, Stud?"

"Absolutely." Nope, but Connor had been Beck's friend, so he needed to be calm. "Holler if there are things we need for the little ones."

Beck took him inside, where another one of Beck's buddies was already taking apart the safety cage around Connor's wood stove.

"Hey, Beck. I'm really sorry, man."

"Thanks, Logan. And that's a good call, we're definitely going to need that."

"I thought so. Have a look at the baby gates Paul stacked up in the kitchen. There's two tall dog-proof ones I thought you could probably use. We have one in our nursery, so we can leave the door open."

They obviously hadn't met Bruiser, who'd learned everything about leaping from Walter.

"Let's take them all. I bet we need them."

The gates were stacked into his truck while he and Beck wandered the house. "Is this really awkward, or is it just me?" Beck asked as he poked his head into Connor's bedroom. "I feel like we're...grave robbing or something."

"It's not cool, but it has to be done, I guess." What was weird was that in a few years, him and Beck would be their daddies, and there wasn't a damn thing that could be done about that. They would know stories about Connor, but that was it.

They'd be good ones, though. He just knew it.

Beck stood in the center of Connor's bedroom, looked around, shook his head, and brushed past him as he left. "Not in here. Not today."

He sighed and gathered the pictures from the bedside table, from the walls. One day these would be priceless.

Beck took toys and kid-sized towels from the bathroom, a music box from a shelf in the hall, a few other things. "Heath said we can come back. I just...can't yet with that stuff. I'm sorry."

"Don't apologize, baby. You don't have to. It's not like we want the man's laundry. I grabbed photos. Don't forget the bubble bath. Charlie was asking for it this morning." They worked hard, grabbing bags and boxes of the kids' things.

An hour or so later, they were all outside, leaning on Heath's truck and his, and Paul had handed out bottles of water.

"So here's the plan, guys. We're going to your house, and we're going to move this stuff in and help you rearrange.

Lunch is already at the house; Jake's wife put it together. Everyone ready?"

Beck looked at Sky as they got back into his truck. "This is...unbelievable. You have to help me figure out how to say thank you."

"You say 'Thank you.' When one of them has a sick baby, we send food. When one moves, we offer to help." Beck could complicate shit quick.

"I guess." Beck nodded. "Doesn't seem like enough. Maybe because this feels...huge. I forget sometimes how great my friends are. And Connor's friends, I guess. Some of them are Connor's friends too."

"Baby, you're a good guy. You are helping Connor's babies in the most huge way possible. They care. You'd have been there if it was one of them? If it was Heath?"

"Yeah, of course." Beck sighed. "I get it. I'm just not used to being this guy. I like being the guy that helps better." He snorted. "I know. Duh."

Sky chuckled softly. "From your lips to God's ears, right? We're going to need a lot of help over the next few days."

Like a shit-ton. Enough that he might have to call in cowboys.

"That, or we don't sleep for a month. Seems like asking for help is a better option." They'd followed Heath all the way home, and when they pulled up, Lacey, both kids, and Bruiser came busting out the front door.

"You're home!" Charlie ran right to him, arms out.

"Hello, Miss Charlie! Have you been good?" He scooped her up and hugged her.

"I am! I'm good. Is that my bed?"

"Yep." Okay, he needed to deal with this. "You want to come see the backyard with me a minute?"

"Okay. What's in the backyard?"

Beck's hands landed on his shoulders and gave them a squeeze. "Love you."

"I love you." They walked back, and he tried to think about how to do this. "Miss Charlie, that was your bed. Do you know why?"

"No. Why?"

"Because your dad had a bad accident, baby girl, and he's gone to heaven. Do you remember heaven, where your momma is?" This sucked, and he hated every second, but he had to do it.

She frowned at him, her eyebrows drawing together. "Daddy went to...to see Mommy with God?"

He nodded. "He did. And he wanted us to take care of you and your brother here, so we brought your toys and your bed, and all of Noah's things."

"I want to go too! Cowboy Sky! I want to go to Heaven with them! You keep Noah!"

"I'm sorry, baby. You cain't. That ain't how life works."

"That's not fair! Tell Daddy to come back and get me!" She wriggled to be let go, shoving at his shoulder with her angry little hands.

"It's not fair," he agreed, and he let her down, leaning against the gate. She could be pissed here and not hurt herself. "I'm sorry."

"He promised we'd all be together again. He promised! It's my turn." She crossed her arms and plopped down in the grass.

"He didn't want to die. He wanted to raise y'all up, but he can't." He sat on the grass too, sighing. "It's not fair at all."

"Daddy wants us to live with you?" She looked up, squinting at him.

"He did. Me and Beck are going to give you a room upstairs next to ours."

Charlotte rested her chin in her hands and looked at the grass. After a quiet minute, she sniffled. "I want Daddy." It wasn't a demand; her tone was resigned and sullen. He had a sudden vision, clear as day, of an older girl with chestnut hair and Connor's green eyes sitting right here in the grass with him and crying over something—a boy, maybe—looking to him to make her feel better.

And calling *him* Daddy.

"I'm sorry, baby girl. If you ever need a hug, I promise I will be here to give you one."

She stared at him. "Promise to God?"

"I do." He felt like the words echoed in him like a vow. "I do. I promise to God. If you need me, I'm right here."

She nodded and silently climbed into his lap, leaning hard.

He held her, letting her know that she was in safe arms. He couldn't fix this, but time would. Time, a little love, and maybe puppy kisses.

6

Beck peeled off the last of the painter's tape protecting the trim around the windows in the nursery and stepped back to admire their work. Two weeks ago, he'd have sworn that Sky's accident and months of rehab was the hardest and the most rewarding time of his life. But this week—the weight of sorting out Connor's estate coupled with the unexpected joy of these two new kids in the house —this week was running a very close second.

Dealing with Connor's house, storing things for the kids when they got older, scattering Connor's ashes out in Lake Champlain...that had all been really tough. But after that, friends and business associates had come out of the woodwork to help them literally remake their house. Many hands really did make light work. Their study wasn't put together, but the furniture was moved, the kids' room was finished—paint, carpet, everything. And he and Sky had just finished painting the nursery.

And it wasn't mint green.

"Nice work, Stud." He leaned over and kissed Sky on the cheek, careful to miss the little paint smear next to his husband's ear. Touches had been so important this week. He couldn't get enough.

"It looks fine." Sky smiled at him, and the expression was exhausted, but that smile went all the way up to his husband's eyes. "We just need to move the furniture where we want it and hang pictures."

"Sky? Beck?" Lacey called them from downstairs. They'd basically hired her for the foreseeable future, she'd been by every day this week for at least a few hours. "Lunch is ready!"

"Lunch first. Furniture later." Maybe another day. They needed a break.

"Sounds like a plan." Sky headed down, and Charlotte leapt into his arms as soon as she saw him.

"Cowboy!"

"My Charlie." Sky hugged her tight.

"Lacey, you are amazing. Thank you for making lunch."

"Charlotte helped. She brought me things from the fridge, and she decided we needed grapes and put them in a bowl for us."

"Grapes are my favorite."

"Oh, yeah? I like them too." He grinned. He didn't say it, but everything was Charlotte's favorite.

Noah was zooming around in his play yard. "Hey, Noah! Are you having fun in baby jail?"

"I run!" Noah called back and made another circle.

"*Vroom*, buddy." Sky chuckled and shook his head. "After naps, we'll go spend some quality time in the backyard, y'all. We can play ball."

"Or play keep the ball away from Bruiser. His favorite game." Beck laughed. Bruiser never tired of that one.

"So," Lacey set a flyer down on the kitchen counter as they sat to eat. "It's October. You guys probably don't know this, but Shelburne has an amazing Halloween parade, and downtown Burlington does trick or treating that's super easy for the little ones."

"Oh. Halloween." Wow. He hadn't even looked at a calendar all week.

"Trick or Treat!" Charlotte called out, mouth full. "Like on *Paw Patrol*!"

What the heck was *Paw Patrol*?

"We'll have to run to the store and find costumes, then." Sky grinned at Charlotte. "I want to be Marshall, the construction dog."

"No. No, you are Cowboy Sky."

"Yes, ma'am." Sky rolled his eyes and grabbed a grape.

Beckett laughed. "What am I, Charlie?"

"You're...Walter!"

He snorted. "Walter?"

Charlie giggled, pleased with herself.

"Oh, we're so getting him a tail and ears. Little whiskers. He'll be so cute." Sky waggled his eyebrows madly, making Noah laugh so hard he fell on his butt.

"Oh, we are?" Beckett made a face, and Charlie pointed at him.

"See? Grumpy! Like Walter!"

"I am not grumpy like Walter." He poked her tummy and she giggled more. Was he grumpy? He was trying not to be, especially around the kids. He was going to have to watch that.

She made a fierce little face at him, and it turned into a goofy grin. "That's you. Then there's Cowboy Sky who is like Bruiser!" She grinned hugely, tongue hanging out the side.

"She has a point, Sky. So, does that make you like Violet, girlie?" He made a fishy face, little swimming motions with his hands, and crossed his eyes.

"No!" She grinned and pushed at him. "I can't be a fish."

"Actually," Lacey said, tapping her plate to get her to eat more. "You could totally be a fish for Halloween I bet, or maybe a mermaid!"

Charlie looked at her, eyes going wide. "A mermaid. Ooh."

"You would make a lovely mermaid. Do you know what Noah wants to be?" Sky asked.

She looked over her shoulder at Noah and back at Sky. "Also a cowboy."

Beckett barely stifled his laugh. He had this awful feeling Sky was going to be a cowboy for Halloween for the next ten years. "Yeehaw, Sky."

"Sounds perfect. You gonna be a cowboy with me, Sonny Jim?" Sky scooped the little boy up and snuggled him. "We'll be the best cowboy buddies ever."

Everyone said cowboys made great fathers, and he knew Sky would be, but this was still a little unexpected. Sky had adjusted so quickly. He went from angry to full-on dad in a handful of days. Beck was still processing things. He knew he'd be right there with Sky soon, but in the meantime, he kind of understood why Charlotte thought he was...like Walter.

"Thanks for the flyer and the info, Lacey. We don't really have our fingers on the kid-related activities yet."

"Well, it's hard. They're not in school yet. Once that happens, you'll know about everything."

"I like school! A, B, D, C!" Charlotte had more energy in her little finger...

"Do you? Excellent. Soon you'll be in pre-K, and you'll be so big." Sky sat with Noah, closing his eyes a second.

"Lacey, could you...?"

She gave him a knowing smile and went to grab Noah. "I know somebody who needs a change and a nap."

"Me." Beck nodded. "That's me. I need a nap."

Charlotte shook her head. "Big boys don't take naps, silly."

"You'd be surprised." He scooped her off her stool. "Speaking of nap time..."

"Will you read me a story?"

"I will. You can even pick it." He and Lacey swept the kids out of the room, leaving Sky there to rest. "Be right back, Stud."

Sky grunted in response, making Charlotte giggle again.

Charlotte picked a short book and Noah went into his crib like a dream. "Sleep well, girlie." He patted her arm and she smiled at him and rolled over.

"Noah's a good sleeper, huh?"

Lacey nodded as they went down the stairs. "He's always been pretty quiet. Really easy. You go sit. I'm going to clean up the kitchen."

"You don't have to—"

"Beckett. Go sit."

"Schooled by the babysitter. Wow." He chuckled and went to sit with Sky.

"Nanny. I like nanny better for my résumé," she called after him, and honestly, he did too.

Sky was sitting right where Beck had left him, snoring softly. He watched a minute, just because he could. His husband was so handsome and looked peaceful and young dozing there. Sky would always be beautiful to him.

Damn, this had been a tough week. Maybe they could get into the hot tub tonight.

With the baby monitor.

He sat carefully and hooked an arm over Sky's shoulders.

"Everything okay?" Sky didn't open his eyes. He barely moved his lips.

"Yeah," he whispered, settling into the couch and tucking Sky against him. "Everything is good. It doesn't get much better than this, right here."

7

Two cowboys, one mermaid, and a rainbow cat walked out of their house.

Lord, they'd become the beginning of a bad joke.

Sky looked over the hood of the fancy-assed new SUV and grinned. "Happy Halloween?"

"Smile, cowboy. You're not the one in the cat ears." At some point in the last week as they were pulling costumes together, Beck had shifted from a wary kitty to a flamboyant feline. "Say it with me, fish-girl!"

"Happy Halloween!" They shouted. Beck scooped her up and stuck her in her car seat, laughing. "Much better."

He cracked up and popped Noah in his seat. "Let's go, buddy. We'll have fun."

Sky's back was killing him, his hip hurt, and he was tired, but there was nothing—nothing—that would make him miss this. He was going to video it all.

Beck started up their shiny new ride. "Our first family outing, right? This'll be good. I put the strollers in the car with the diaper bag. Are we forgetting anything?"

"I have no idea." The entire car seemed to be filled with shit for "in case."

"Me neither. Let's do this." They left the driveway, the sweet ride way more comfortable than his truck or Beckett's Jeep already. "It's chilly out. Do you have your long johns on, cowboy?"

"Nah. I just got my good socks." He'd be okay. He wanted Beck to look at his butt. They hadn't had sex in a couple of weeks, and he sort of doubted they ever would again, but he wanted Beck to miss it.

"Noah. Say trick or treat, Noah." Charlie had been trying to get Noah to say it all week. It was getting closer.

"Ticky teat," Noah replied.

"T-r-ick."

Noah giggled. "T-r-cik."

"T-r-eat."

"Ticky teat!" That might be the best she was gonna get.

"Y'all are going to be the best tricky-treaters at the parade. Swear to God." He was about to die of cuteness.

Beck turned on the radio, then reached over and took his hand and gave him a smile. "We get to be parents today. A couple again. A family."

They did, and it was as wonderful as it was terrifying. He still wasn't certain he knew how to do this. He was sure trying, though.

"We can do this." Beck squeezed his hand. "It's going to be fun. Breathe."

"I'm looking forward to it. I can't wait." He had his phone charged up. "Your mom wants pictures."

And to come to Thanksgiving.

"Of course she does. Her grandchild count nearly doubled overnight, and she's so excited. The boys are all superheroes this year, she said."

There was rarely any traffic on their route but today, the streets around Burlington were busy with cars full of kiddos and parents looking for parking. They got to cheat, though, and park in the little private lot Beck leased for the law office.

"We are spoiled rotten. I love it." He stole a quick kiss and went to grab their baby boy. "Bubba, don't eat your cowboy hat."

"My brother eats *everything*." Charlie's eye roll was epic, three going on thirteen.

Noah was all smiles and reached for his hat, but he pulled away right before the little fingers got hold of the brim. "Cow-oo-boy."

Beck sat a stroller next to him and went to get the other. He and Beck had originally planned on Charlie walking, but Lacey explained how heavy a tired, cranky three-year-old would be and they were easily convinced to change their minds.

They were going to need to figure out what to do when the new baby came. Well, other than panic. Charlie wasn't acknowledging that there might be another baby.

Beck-the-Cat stuffed the diaper bag into the little sling on the back of Noah's stroller and slung Charlie's umbrella stroller over one shoulder. "Everybody ready?"

He squinted at Beck. Beck looked ready. Beck was smiling and holding Charlie's hand and looked a hundred percent like a capable dad. Was that real or just a good show? His husband had the same tired circles under his eyes that he did, but he seemed to have double the energy.

Hell, maybe he was just getting old. Sky sure as shit felt older than he had.

Noah patted his cheeks. "Papa."

"Hmm?"

"Papa. Papa cow-boy."

Oh, that was something. Papa, huh? He thought he'd be a daddy, but he'd be whatever they needed him to be. "That's right, son. You and your papa are cowboys, through and through."

Beck let him push Noah and hooked an arm through his. "So, how many times do you think you'll get asked for pictures? Should we make a bet?"

"I'm voting on none. There's a ton of costumes, and I'm not even dressed up." He had his rodeoing clothes on, and his jeans still fit.

"Oh, yeah you are." Beck walked a little closer, just long enough to say, "Don't tell me you don't know how hot you are in those jeans."

Maybe a little bit, sure. All he did was wink over and give Beck his best pirate smile.

"Uh-huh. Stud." Beck winked back at him and led the way to the parade.

It wasn't hard to find. They lucked into a spot out of the wind where they could see pretty well. Beck stuck Charlie up on his shoulders and held on to her feet as they waited for things to get under way.

Noah held up his little hands. "Papa! Me too!"

"Okay, Bubba, hold up." He shook his head and picked Noah up, propping him up on his chest facing out.

"His name is Noah," Charlie informed him, and he nodded.

"But he's your bubba, just like you're his big sister."

"He's Bubba and you're Papa?" Charlie looked confused but determined to figure this out. "What about, him?" Charlie bopped Beckett on the head and Beck winced.

"What about me?"

"What's your name?" Charlie might as well have added, "Duh."

"Uh...Beckett?"

"What do you want to call him, Sister? If I get to be y'all's papa, who is he?" *Please, little girl, don't hurt him. He's trying so hard.*

She scrunched her little face up. "Papa and...Pappy?"

Oh, these were little redneck babies, no matter where they came from. He loved it. "What do you think, Pappy?"

Beckett reached up high and ruffled her hair. "Sounds great, little girlie." Beck leaned over so she could give Sky a little peck on the cheek.

"Oh, you guys are so cute. Can I get a picture?" A young mom with a baby in a backpack stopped right in front of him. "Look at that little cowboy hat!"

He heard Beck chuckle and could just imagine the look on his husband's face.

He quirked his lips, tipped his hat to her, and winked. "Ma'am."

Noah cackled and kicked, and they leaned into Beck a little. So they were doing this. This was their first Halloween with kids. "Could you take a picture of us with my phone, please?"

"Oh, yeah. For sure." She stuffed her phone into her pocket and took his.

Beck stepped up close behind him with an arm around his waist, hand resting on his hip. "Smile, girlie!"

Above him, he heard Charlie say, "Cheese!"

Noah crowed and waved at her, then went back to doing...whatever his odd, goofy little boy was doing in his head. Sky couldn't wait to find out what that was.

"So sweet. Congrats, you guys." She handed him his phone.

"I guess that was our first family photo, huh?" Beck drummed those long fingers on the top of his hat, playfully.

Then the Halloween music started, and a float with the Addams Family on it rolled toward them.

"Pappy..." Charlie didn't sound convinced this was a good idea. "Pappy, are they mean? They look mean."

"No, sweetie. They're just meant to be a spooky-looking family. They're actually pretty funny." Beck jostled her and brilliantly moved her attention to the witch throwing candy into the crowd off the back of a pickup instead. "Catch, baby! Try to catch one!"

Sky caught a couple, and one landed on his hat. He slipped them to Beck, just to help. Beck squeezed his fingers as he took them.

"Charlie! Papa's hat!"

She reached forward and grabbed it, brandishing in the air like a trophy. "I got one!"

"You did, look at you!" Beck pretended to catch one and handed it to Charlie. "Good job, baby."

"Me too Papa! Me too!"

"Pappy will catch one for you." He realized, all of the sudden, that he didn't know what candy was safe for a one-and-a-half-year-old.

Beck pulled out a tiny baggy of Goldfish out of nowhere and put it in Sky's hand. It was like they had a system, when really, all they had was instinct.

"Here's one, Bubba!" He put a Goldfish in Noah's little hand.

"Catch, Papa!"

"That's right, Bubba. Catch." At least that's what he thought Noah said. It was always a bit of a guess.

Over the next twenty minutes, there were dinosaurs and superheroes, storybook characters and creatures from kids'

TV shows he'd been known to watch before Beck woke up on Saturday mornings. Noah got itchy being held right about the time the crowd jumped in at the end of the parade, and both kids ended up in strollers by the time they'd gone three blocks.

Luckily, in three blocks was a little coffee shack with caramel hazelnut lattes, plus juices for the little ones.

Beck held up his cup. "We are rocking this parade thing, Stud. How do you feel?"

"I was sore when we started, but I'm loosening up." This was charming as hell, the kids were being decent, and Beck made him smile. "Hot tub post getting everyone to bed?"

"There is literally nothing I want more right now than you in the hot tub." Beck's look made him feel seen, despite all the crowd and the kids and how busy they'd been. "So we'll make it happen."

"Rock on." They let Charlie trick-or-treat until she was worn out. Noah was already asleep, holding his hat in both hands. He snapped a quick picture, then looked down at Charlie. "You ready to go home, Sister?"

She yawned and shook her head no but didn't actually answer the question.

"We can walk slowly, sweetie." Beck turned the stroller around. "Come on, Stud. Pappy's ready. This has been great, though. You got good pictures for Mom?"

"I did, plus a video of Bubba going 'Ticky teat!' and one of Charlie being brave and shaking Wednesday's hand." He chuckled softly. Those were priceless. Jesus, he didn't understand how his had life moved so fast, but he was grateful as hell for it.

"So mean." Beck reached over and smoothed a hand across his shoulders. "Have I mentioned how good you look today? I know most people think that's a costume, but I know better. You look like my cowboy."

"I am yours." They wandered out, gathering a few more little toys and a couple more chocolate bars on the way to the cars.

"I'm going to get her in the car. You think you can get Noah into his seat without waking him up?"

"If I can't, I'll jostle him back to sleep." Weren't kids supposed to like sleeping in the car?

He managed to settle Noah in, snuggling him in with a blanket.

It wasn't until they were in the car and Beck closed the door that Beck looked tired. He sighed and rested his forehead on the steering wheel. "Damn. I'm ready for that hot tub, baby."

"You want me to drive home? I can." This vehicle was cushy as hell and easy to drive.

Beck looked over at him. "Yeah? I wouldn't say no if you're serious."

"Sure, baby. I don't mind at all. You want to zip through somewhere and grab a burger?"

"Also a great idea." Beck hopped out to trade places with him. "I didn't realize I was hungry until you mentioned it."

"Yeah, I am craving a heart attack in a bag." Sky got the seat changed, and he had to admit, he loved the whole "push a button and the seats and mirrors adjust to you" bit. "I loved that—the parade and sh—shtuff. That was cool."

"Shtuff." Beck chuckled. "It was pretty neat. And the kids were so good."

"Yeah. Pappy. That was..." He glanced to make sure she was asleep. "I was worried. Noah, no. He don't remember a thing, but her?"

"I know. I'm still worried. But at least we weren't total

strangers, you know? I just...I feel like I'm waiting for the other shoe to drop. This was a good day, though."

"Yeah." The other shoe? There were going to be a shit-ton of shoes pelting them. They were just on their best goddamn behavior and praying that the good Lord took pity on them, and Sky knew it.

"Pappy is cute." Beck gave him a tired smile. "I had no idea...I like that you asked her."

Lord, he'd just been glad she didn't short out and scream like a banshee. "I didn't know what else to do. I mean, we cain't expect her to call us daddy or nothing, and this is... this is special. When little bit comes, she'll know her brother and sister named us."

"She or he," Beck teased. "Although I feel like I should believe you." Beck looked into the back seat. "Is it me, or does part of you keep thinking you're going to wake up tomorrow and laugh about having had this crazy dream?"

"It's not you. I dreamed a couple nights ago that I'd died in that hospital, and this whole thing was a dream."

Beck reached for him, fingers landing on his thigh. "If that's the case, I say we don't wake up."

"Fair enough." He turned into the drive-thru and ordered them burgers, fries, and milkshakes.

"Oh, good call on the milkshake."

It was a good call, and they were both gone, noisy straws sucking up the last drops before he pulled into their driveway.

"I'll grab the food and the boy, you get the girl and our new fancy baby purse?"

Beck nodded, laughing. "I'm on it."

He could hear Charlie complaining softly as they moved inside, and Beck's low, soothing voice. Beck left Charlie on the couch in what was now their office. "You want me to see if he'll go down upstairs? She's going to be hungry soon, I bet."

"Yeah. I may get a chocolate milk in her, at least." She didn't want to be up when she wasn't ready. At all.

Beck took the baby, who snuggled right in like sleeping was the best thing ever. "I think I'm jealous of him." Beck grinned and gave him a quick kiss. "I'll be right back."

"Hey, Mergirl. You want some chocolate milk, Sister? Do you need to potty?"

She looked up at him, frowning deeply. "I want my daddy."

Poor baby. "I know, honey. I'm sorry."

"No." She pushed at his hand as he tried to touch her hair, and she rolled over.

"Okay." He wasn't going to fight with her. He went outside and turned on the hot tub, then came in to put the burgers out on the table.

"Smells good." Beck reappeared, having ditched the cat costume, wearing sweats and a T-shirt, and warm hands circled his waist. "Charlie is still out?"

"She's having a pout. I'm letting her do it." If Beck wanted to try, he could, but he didn't know what else to do.

"Seems like the wise thing to do." Beck turned him and danced him out of the kitchen. "I know we should eat, but I'm celebrating five childless minutes."

"Five whole minutes? Wow." He rested his cheek against Beck's shoulder.

"Hey, if there is anything I've learned in the last few weeks, it's take it when you can get it." There was no music playing, and Beck wasn't setting a particular rhythm, but it didn't matter—they were swaying together, and Beck was holding him close. It was still dancing. "You feel good."

"I do. I started the hot tub up." He had to smile at Beck's little bounce. Someone wanted to be an adult for a minute.

Had to be the jeans.

"Oh, I can't wait. It'll be toasty after we get Charlie in bed."

"I don' wanna go to bed. I'm hungry." Charlie hugged her arm around one of his legs, and Beck slowed to a light sway.

Beck smiled down at her. "Papa told me he has chocolate milk."

"Okay." She sounded tired and pouty, but she was cooperating.

"Do you want peanut butter toast? Or an egg? Some of my hamburger?"

She craned her neck to look up at him. "Egg?"

"Egg, *please*," Beck said gently.

"Please egg, Papa?"

"Yes, ma'am." She only ate them scrambled, so he didn't have to ask that. "You want to crack it for me, or you want me to deal with it, sweet girl?"

Her eyes went wide. "Me!"

"Oh, you're a brave one, Papa." Beckett reluctantly let him go, hands lingering at his beltline a second longer, then followed them into the kitchen.

"We got this." They had a weird little rhythm to this. Plastic bowl, extra egg, rag, chair for standing on—all the important bits to making an egg.

Beckett watched them as he and Charlie made their mess, cleaned it up, and put a perfectly acceptable egg on the stove.

"It's *easy*, Pappy." There was that eye roll again. Those tween years were going to be fun. "See?"

"I had no idea. I thought it was hard." Beckett made a point of sounding very impressed.

"You could do it too." Charlie nodded. "You could."

"Yeah?" Beck smiled at her. "Well, next time you can teach me."

She looked to him, eyes wide. "Can I?"

"Sure, baby. You can so teach him. He's smart as a whip, like you."

She beamed at him, so proud, and helped him stir her egg.

"You need anything on your burger, baby?" Beckett went to the fridge and came back with a jar of pickles.

"I'm good with it as is, thanks." Sky got her down and in her little booster seat deal, a cup of chocolate milk and a plate of eggs in front of his girl. "Here we go. Did you have the best day?"

Charlie nodded, talking with her mouth full. "I saw dinosaurs and Spider-Man and Wednesday was nice and not mean. And she was pretty. Can I have my candy?"

"Two pieces. That's all or you won't sleep, girlie." Beck brought over the little bag for her to dig through.

"This is Pappy's." She held out a mini Hershey bar for Beckett, and he took it with a smile.

"Thank you, Charlie."

She dug around some more until she came up with another one and held it out to him. "This is yours, Papa."

"That's my favorite, sweet love. Thank you." He couldn't stop smiling at her, swear to God. "Which two are you going to pick?"

"Kit Kat and...this one."

"Three Musketeers. Good choice." Beckett's favorite, in fact. He knew it well. "So you'll eat those, and then we'll get you tucked in, okay? It's been a big day, you need your beauty sleep."

"Beauty sleeps?" She blinked up at Beckett, eyes wide, and Sky fought the urge to cackle.

"Oh sure," Beckett said as if he knew what he was talking about. "When you don't get enough sleep you start to look like Wednesday. Pale and big circles under your eyes. Sleep is very important."

"Oh..." She stared at him like he was serious. "I sleep."

No laughing. None.

Beckett winked at him and scooped her up, taking her upstairs as she ate her chocolate. "That's my smart girl. Do you know what book you want to read?"

Sky didn't hear her answer, and it didn't matter. He cleaned up the dishes and ate his candy bar. He was one tired son of a bitch, but they'd managed Halloween one without hysteria.

Beck came back down with a smile, carrying the baby monitor, which he set on the kitchen counter. "I totally rocked bedtime."

"It was a decent day, wasn't it? She seemed to have fun." And so did Noah, although fun was way easier with him. He was pre-happy for his convenience.

"She asked me if we could do it again tomorrow, so yeah. I think she enjoyed it." Beck started to knead his shoulders with warm, strong hands. "How are you holding up?"

"I'm good. I'm ready for our bubble, but..." He shrugged one shoulder. "It was a good night, baby. That was neat."

"It was, right? Fun. Something to look forward to doing again next year. With the baby. We're going to have our hands full." Beck kissed the side of his neck.

"Yeah. I hope I can figure it out. Three babies...I still can't look at it head on, you know?"

"Nope. Me neither. But it's happening, so we'll figure that out like we figure everything else out. Together."

"Yeah." He hauled himself up off the counter and went to take a kiss.

Sky got one, his Beck coming on strong in a way he hadn't in forever. Beck's arm caught him tight around the waist, and one hand rested along his jaw. *Oh, hell.* That was what he needed. A second of heat, a little bit of need—he craved that bad.

Beck broke the kiss, lips moving to his neck and down to his shoulder, fingers pulling aside the fabric of his shirt to reveal his skin. "You smell like this guy I have the hots for."

"Do I? You sure about that?" Sky did love it when Beck seduced him. It wasn't like it was hard to do, but it sure was fun.

"Yeah, pretty sure. He likes it when I do this." Beck's tongue found his collarbone and traced it. "And this." Beck's lips closed over the soft spot just above it and sucked on it, not quite hard enough to leave a mark, but enough for him to feel it.

His fingers found Beck's ass, and he squeezed, dragging them harder together. He could feel the ridge of Beck's cock, pressed against him, and it made him groan.

Beck took two steps, moving him back to the counter and rocked into him. "Hey, Stud. Remember me?"

"Every fucking second of the day. Yes." With all his heart.

"Yeah. Been a while, though." Beck lifted him and sat his butt on the counter, looking into his eyes. "I need you."

"Take me, I'm yours." He took a hard, happy kiss, diving into Beck's hungry lips.

Beck's fingers started to work his fly open but froze suddenly.

The realization that Beck couldn't just have him right

there in the kitchen anymore could have been a hell of a buzzkill, but Beck took a breath and managed to save the moment. His husband's lips hovered close to his, and whispered, "You pour the wine, and I'll grab our robes."

Beck lifted him off the counter again and set him on his feet.

Weirdly, the fact that Beck had helped Sky keep his mind in the middle was the sexiest goddamn thing ever. It felt...special and new, in the best sort of way.

"I'm on it." Two acrylic glasses of Cab, a baby monitor, and the radio—he was good to go.

Beck came back wearing a robe and carrying his. "Slip that on, cowboy. I'll meet you out there." Beck left the robe with him and went to light the hurricane candles on the deck.

He stripped in the laundry room, put on his flip-flops and his robe, and headed out. Handing Beck his wine, he lost his robe and slid into the water.

"Mmm. Now that's what I want. A little wine and an armful of my cowboy." Beck hooked an arm over his shoulders and tugged him closer. "How's the hip? You looked a little stiff climbing in here."

"Better than I was before our evening. We walked out a little stiffness, you know?" His own pun made him chuckle. Lord, he was a dipshit, but he did amuse himself.

"Funny, mine seemed to become more...acute. I appreciate that you broke out those jeans for me, they fit you just right." Beck took a sip of wine and hummed happily. "Just right."

"I'll keep that in mind." Anything for that lovely attention. Anything at all. "I wouldn't do this with no one but you."

"This." Beck kissed his temple. "This, what? Sit naked in a hot tub?"

"This be a father. This be a husband. This sit naked in a hot tub." It was one and all. He didn't want to do it without Beck.

Beck caught his gaze and held it. "There is no one else I *could* do any of this with. You're the only one. *This*...all of this, takes trust. A kind of trust I only have in you. My faith in us is strong, Sky." His husband's eyes twinkled. "I only want to sit naked in a hot tub with you."

"Good. I don't share." That hadn't changed one bit.

"I don't know what you're so jealous of. Just because Noah spit up on me three times today and only once on you doesn't mean he loves you any less." Beck gave him a sideways grin. "Honestly."

"Are you sure?" He fluttered his eyelashes outrageously as he let himself float over to settle on Beck's lap, hand "accidentally" landing on that pretty prick. "Are you real sure?"

He could see the goose bumps, hear his husband's sharp inhale even over the rumble of the jets. "Nope." Beck shook his head. "I don't remember a goddamn thing all of a sudden."

"Uh-huh." He leaned in, lips brushing the line of Beck's jaw, as he dragged his fingers up the fat shaft and circled the tip.

Beck dipped his chin and caught his lips in a kiss, a hot tongue teasing them open. One hand found his ass and the other set his wineglass down on the wide ledge surrounding the hot tub. Fuck, he wanted this—all of it, every inch, every touch, everything.

Beck's hands explored his skin, gliding under the water, finding his muscle and his soft spots, reminding them both how real he was, how solid. Teeth found his earlobe and fingers found his nipples, standing at attention in the cool night air. "Love you."

"Love." Fuck, Sky's eyes crossed, and his fingers tightened, squeezing a little harder than normal, making Beck gasp. "Sorry, babe."

"Uh-huh. Just don't stop." Beck shifted him slightly, making room to get his fingers around Sky's prick too, and picked up the rhythm, long strokes matching Sky's every move.

His eyelids went heavy, his lips parting. "Not. Won't. Fuck, Beck."

Oh, that was not coherent. Not at all.

Whatever Beck mumbled in agreement wasn't either, so it was all good. They kissed and stroked each other, sounds muffled by the bubbling water, steam rising around them as the night air grew colder.

"Sky, I want...I need...more."

He knew it was coming, he knew his husband so well. Beck pressed the bottle of lube into his hand, planted one foot, and levered them up and out of the water. They'd done this so many times.

Not recently—a couple of weeks at least, but it felt like it had been forever.

It was easy to slick himself up, press his lubed fingers deep before he dragged the lube along Beck's shaft and, not wasting any time, joined their bodies together.

He loved this—the sensation of heat filling him, the cold on his upper body that was damn near painful, the comfort of his lover's arms.

"Sky." Beck settled them back down into the water, easing the chill as he got comfortable. It didn't matter that he was riding; Beck wouldn't be still, rocking under him, working his cock with a steady, knowing hand.

"Tell me we get to do this together forever." He never wanted to lose Beck's need, his passion.

"Forever," Beck growled, teeth closing down hard on his shoulder. His body tightened in a rush, that sting enough to take him from zero to sixty.

"Do it again." He didn't need much. Not at all.

"Yeah. Right with you, cowboy." Beck found another spot and licked it first, then bit, teeth bruising into his skin.

He shot so hard he swore his bones rattled, and he fought the urge to yell with everything he had. Not a second later, Beck grabbed him by the hips and bucked up, and he felt the pulsing and the heat of his husband spilling inside him.

He leaned back, letting the water and Beck buoy him. "D-damn. Damn, baby."

"Mmm. That was just what the doctor ordered, right? I do love you, cowboy." Beck touched and stroked and soothed him with gentle, affectionate fingers.

"Perfect. Fucking perfect." He couldn't stop his head from bobbing, the orgasm and hot water together making him stupid.

"Let's see if we can finish our wine without being interrupted. Then I'll take you inside for a shower." Beck maneuvered him easily in the water and sat him down before handing him his glass. "Pretty soon there will be snow out here."

"Yes. Thanksgiving. Christmas. New Year's. New baby." It was going to zoom by. He couldn't believe how fast it all was.

"Sierra or Dalton." Beck sipped his wine. "Not to ruin the mood, but Mom and Dad want to come for Thanksgiving."

"I think they should. They need to meet Charlie and Noah before the baby comes. It's only fair." Beck's dad would learn to cope with him, dammit, come hell or high water. It would happen.

"Yeah? I do too, but I wasn't sure how you'd feel about it. I thought maybe we could put them up in that cute B and B up the road. Close enough but...not here." Beck grinned.

"Not until we finish the basement and make it functional as a guest room. I don't want to hear about how it's a wreck." Maybe he'd get Parker to come help him work on the damn thing....

Beck chuckled. "You know my parents well. Plus, this way they'll have breakfast there, and you know my dad. He doesn't get out the door before ten, ever. So we'll have quiet mornings."

"And if your mom wants, I'll pick her up and bring her over earlier. You know that." Sometimes he wondered what his folks would think about this—his family.

"I know. She loves you. She's going to love the kids." Beck pointed at the sky. "Shooting star. Did you see it?"

"Did you make a wish?" How many times had he asked that question in his life? Now he would teach the kids to ask it, and one day, his grandbabies would ask it.

"I didn't. All my wishes have already come true."

"We got one left to wish for. Healthy and whole and home." He needed their last kiddo born safe and healthy.

"True. Keep watching, we can catch the next one." Beck lifted his face to the stars, eyes catching the moonlight.

"Sounds like a plan. We'll share the next one."

8

"Sky? That book...Connor's book. Is there a pediatrician in it?" Noah woke them early and had been fussing and crying since before dawn. Beckett was holding him with one arm, bouncing him slightly as he dug through a box of baby supplies they hadn't unpacked yet, looking for a thermometer. "He has a fever, I think. We should maybe take him in. What does a baby thermometer even look like?"

Charlotte reached into the box and pulled out a weird handheld thing with a digital readout and held it to him. "This goes in his ear."

Beck blinked at her. "In his ear?"

She demonstrated on her own ear and after a second the thing beeped cheerfully, the display turning green and reading 98.4. She held it out to him again. "Green is good."

"Green is good, huh? Thank you, sweetie." *Jesus Christ.* He'd been saved by a three-year-old.

He held the gadget in Noah's ear. Noah protested like Beck was trying to kill him, and the display turned red.

"Red is *bad*," Charlie said in a doomsday voice. "Noah is sick."

Sky wandered in, took Noah, handed him the "baby manual," squirted a dropperful of red stuff into the baby's mouth, and popped a sippy cup in there before Noah could cry. "Rock on, Charlie. You are the world's best big sister."

He stared at Sky, who shrugged. "Figured they're like horses. Don't warn them."

"What was in the dropper?" He started flipping through the book. "Should I call the doctor? Or should we go right to the ER?" He looked up at Sky. "Aren't you worried? Why don't you look worried?"

"Baby Tylenol. And he's not running like a temperature of a thousand, but it's a fever, so you should call, but nothing is running out of any hole, there's no blood, and he's drinking, so that's good, right?" God save him from practical cowboys who treated children like livestock.

"There's no blood..." he muttered, finding the doctor's number and pulling out his cell phone and dialing. "Are you serious?" Sky was a bull rider; he probably wouldn't be worried if there was blood either. "We have baby Tylenol?"

He ended up in a phone tree. "Oh. Press two to speak to a nurse..." he pressed two and waited.

"We have baby Tylenol, plus that juice stuff if one of them does start running from the butt end." Sky nuzzled Noah. "Bubba, your pappy is a giant dorkus-malorkus, but he's cute, so we'll keep him."

"Papa, what's a dorkus-malorkus?" Charlie asked, and Sky tilted his head, blinked, then pointed at Beckett.

"Him. The cutest one ever. Wanna come brush Bruiser while Pappy helps your brother?"

Sky was no help. None.

The nurse came on, very kindly did not laugh at him when he explained the situation, and told him to call back if the fever stayed up. Otherwise, he might be teething or have a bug.

He hung up and stared at his phone. "She basically told me to chill out in kind doctor-speak."

"Dorkus-malorkus!" Charlie called out and sauntered past him. "You're cute, Pappy."

"Thanks." He followed her to find Noah half-dozing in Sky's arms. As soon as Noah saw him, though, those little legs started kicking.

"Pappy! Want Pappy!"

He smiled. He hadn't realized Noah had picked up on the name too. "Oh, buddy. I'm right here." He plucked Noah out of Sky's arms. "You're okay. Go back to sleep. Dorkus-malorkus will save you from the cold-hearted cowboy."

"That's me." Sky grabbed Charlie and danced with her. "Cold as ice."

"No, Papa." She patted his cheeks. "You're warm. You're always warm."

Sky chuckled. "Maybe we should have chicken noodle soup for supper. That would be good for your bubba."

"With elbows!"

"Elbows can be arranged." Beck had Noah settled on one shoulder, eyes drooping again. "Do you know, she said it could be his teeth?"

"Yeah? Aren't they all there yet?" Sky looked at Charlie. "Want to go to the Walmart with me, baby girl? We can get stuff for soup, Baby Orajel, and pick out a new toy."

She frowned at him. "One for Bubba?"

"Yes, ma'am. And we'll get something for the new baby." Sky was trying hard to ease Charlie into the idea of another sibling.

"New baby doesn't need anything. They're still in that lady's tummy." Charlie rolled her eyes.

"Charlie, do you like to pick out clothes? Because Papa and I have to pick something out for the baby to wear home from the hospital, and I don't know if we'll be good at it."

Sky shot him an "Oh, good one" look over Charlie's head.

"Do you know if it's a brother or a sister?" she asked. Again.

"Not yet. We want to be surprised," Sky told her.

"Why?"

"Because surprises are great."

"Papa. You know it's a baby." Oh, the literalism was strong with this one.

"Lacey told me people buy yellow and green things when they don't know if it's a boy or a girl. What do you think? Or, you could pick out one of each. Then we'd have both." He gave her a wink.

"I want the baby to come home in a dinosaur outfit."

"Oh?" Sky grinned and nodded. "I love that. Want to come with me? Leave Pappy and Bubba here?"

Charlie nodded and ran for her shoes, and Sky winked at him. "I figured you two could have hard snuggles. You need anything else from the store, baby?"

"You are a brilliant man. And I'm totally down with a dinosaur outfit." Beck kissed his cheek. "Oreos."

"Right on. Oreos. Chicken-soup stuff. Goodies. Laundry detergent. I'm a shopping machine."

They'd become so domestic. A couple of regular dads. "I'm going to sit here with the sick boy for a while. Then I'm going see if I can't get him to sleep so I can start putting the baby's crib together."

"Good deal. Don't stress it. I won't be long." Sky came over and gave him a quick kiss. "Love you."

"Love you, Stud."

"Love you too, stud, bye!" Charlie stuck her lips out for a kiss, and Beck chuckled as he gave her a quick smooch.

"Be good for Papa."

He watched Sky bustle her out the door, and the house went quiet. Really quiet. And still. Noah snorted softly and settled in even harder, sound asleep.

He woke up to soft giggles, the smell of cooking and coffee, and a heavy blanket covering him.

"Can I give Noah a grape, Papa?"

"Sure, baby girl."

He blinked his eyes open feeling a little disoriented. Noah wasn't with him anymore, and he was lying down. He remembered stretching out with Noah on his chest....He must have closed his eyes. "Home already?" Whoa, that sounded like a frog croaking through a pillow. He cleared his throat and tried again. "How was shopping?"

"We had a ball. We bought some Christmas presents, we picked out a wooden puzzle for Noah, a set of neat blocks for Charlie, and a dragon outfit for the new baby."

"And we buyed chickens and carrots and coffee!"

"Ooh. I can't wait to see your blocks, Charlie." He sat up and ran his fingers through his hair before hauling his ancient butt off the couch. "Do I smell coffee?"

"Pumpkin spice latte, just for you."

Oh, Sky did love him best.

"Papa found rolls and cupcakes for later. And we singed all the way home together."

"What did you sing? Cowboy songs or *Frozen*?" He put both hands around his fancy latte and lifted it to his lips. "Mmm."

"We singed *Moana*. All of it." She brought him a plastic

bag filled with multicolored wooden blocks. It was fascinating to see the toys Sky helped them choose. No electronics. Nothing fancy. Wooden puzzles and blocks and rag dolls. "See. Look. We can build a house."

"I can't wait. Should we build one while Papa is making soup? It smells great, Sky." He set his coffee on the counter and cut a few more grapes into little pieces for Noah, who was looking a little better and making grabby hands.

"Okay. Papa, can you watch the baby?"

"Me and Bubba are fine. We're going to play with his puzzle after a bit."

He let Charlie pull him down onto the rug by the newly gated-off wood stove. Bruiser joined them instantly, curling up behind Charlie and huffing softly to make sure she knew he was there.

Beckett glanced up at Walter, who they only seemed to spend time with in bed these days. Otherwise Walter hung out up high in his cat tree, watching. The poor kitty was still trying to decide how he felt about these tiny, noisy usurpers who'd been stealing his lap time.

At least he'd stopped grumbling and growling.

Meanwhile Bruiser was everybody's best friend.

"Noah looks less pale, huh? You think he's better?"

She nodded, dumping out her blocks. "Papa put goo in his mouth and said he felt something."

"Oh, yeah? Well, maybe it's a new tooth like the doc said. I was worried. I didn't like him being sick." If he was a wreck over a new tooth, what was he going to be like when they had an ear infection or the flu? He wished he had Sky's experience with livestock; maybe he could just pretend they were cows.

Yeah. That was never going to happen.

"How do we start, baby? Like this?" He started goofing around, piling the blocks up high.

"The—the these ones go on top." She pushed a green triangle into his hand. "How do you call these?"

"Green triangle."

"Green triangle. Green is good. On top."

Green is good. Red is *bad*. Remembering the serious little look on her face earlier made him chuckle. And she was right. She was totally right.

"Green on top." He put the triangle on the top of his little stack of blocks. "Like that?"

She nodded and pulled blocks from his pile over to hers; then she began to stack, concentrating so hard.

"That looks good, sweetie, you're doing great." He slowly built a little stack close to hers, thinking they could bridge them in a minute. "What are we building?"

"This is the road to Pappy's house. This is Charlie's house. Now we need Papa's house and Bubba's house."

"Okay." He used a few of the red blocks to make Sky's house. "Papa is going to have a barn. What about Noah?" He was trying, he really was, but "bubba" didn't come out of his mouth naturally. Charlie, on the other hand, picked up the bubba-sister thing like she'd been born in Texas. Beck loved it. There was so little of Sky's culture up here in Vermont, it was good to bring bits of it in where they could.

"He needs a Spider-Man house. He will be Spider-Man when he grows up." Okay, that was sure.

"Has he been bitten by a spider yet? That's how it happens, I hear. Or was he just born spidery?" He looked at the blocks that were left trying to figure out how they would become a Spider-Man house.

That was when Walter decided to come down from his cat tree.

Walter landed on Bruiser and startled him, making the pup scramble between Beck and Charlie. It was loud and nobody got hurt, but Bruiser took out their little village and kicked the blocks all over the family room.

"Whoa, easy, Bruiser!" He tried to calm the dog, but Bruiser was already traumatized.

Charlie screeched and started crying, and Bruiser hid under the blanket on the couch.

Walter sat and gave himself a bath.

"Mean kitty! Bad bad kitty!" she screeched, and Walter just stared at her.

"Whoa." Sky scooped Walter up. "Was he playing with Bruiser again?"

"He's not nice! You spank him. Right now!" She stamped her foot, frowning fiercely.

"No. Hitting critters isn't cool, ladybug. Walter here just wanted to play. He's new to having kiddos around." Sky kept loving on Walter. "Critters count on us, you know. We're here to take care of them, to love them, and help them have good lives. It's important. It's the cowboy way."

"Well, all due respect to the cowboy in residence, I think Walter is kind of the anti-cowboy." He pulled Charlie into his lap. "It would be nice if we could have a conversation with Walter and explain that you guys just want to be friends, right? But we can't. So, we have to show him instead. He's an old kitty is all. He needs a little more time."

Charlie frowned, but she glanced up at Sky. "Okay. I want to be a cowboy."

"I think you will be an amazing cowboy. In fact, why don't you love on Bruiser? He got jumped on. I'll bring Walter in with me for a little bit." Sky leaned close and whispered. "Bruiser thinks you hung the moon or held the ladder for the person who did."

Charlie smiled and climbed up on the couch so carefully. "Hey, Bruiser. Are you okay? It's just me." Bruiser stuck his nose out from under the blanket, licked her fingers, and stuck his head in her lap. She petted his head. "I'm a cowboy. I take care of you."

Beckett hauled himself up off the floor. "Nice work, cowboy." He gave Walter a scritch under the chin. "It's okay, buddy. You'll always be the one who came first."

Walter yowled at him, the sound piteous and long-suffering. Someone needed catnip. Bad.

He leaned over Walter and stole a quick kiss from Sky. "Poor Walter. Let's get him stoned. Charlie said you felt something in Noah's mouth?" He followed Sky into the kitchen, where Noah was strapped into his little booster seat and banging a plastic dinosaur happily against the plastic tray.

"Little teeth back there trying to come out. The Orajel made all the difference." Sky grinned at him. "How was your coffee?"

"Perfect. Fixed me right up." Beckett went for the catnip, which they kept with Walter's treats in a high cabinet. Walter had outsmarted the lower ones. "I learned not to panic until you do. No pressure." He winked.

"Yeah, I'm not smart enough to panic, baby." Sky peeked at the soup, the smell just amazing.

"You saved the day, Stud." He circled his arms around Sky and peered over his husband's shoulder at the soup.

"I just did it like you do. You'll have to do the spice bit. I got Brown 'N Serves to go with. Charlie says they both like them."

"That's a win, huh?" He kissed Sky's neck. Damn, Sky smelled better than the chicken soup. But...Noah tossed the little dinosaur, and it hit him in the ass like a warning. He was going to have to learn how to ride out the buzz for a while.

"I got it, buddy." He galloped it back across the kitchen counter toward Noah, who giggled madly. "Rawr!"

"Pappy! Rawr!" Oh, that was heaven. Right here. Right now. In his kitchen.

9

"I will not!" The chocolate milk went flying, hitting wall and floor and ceiling.

Sky had two options: one, he put Charlie over his knee and blister her little ass; or two, he remove her from his immediate line of sight.

So, he picked her up without a word, put her in her room, and shut the door. Hard.

Then he put Noah in his Pack 'n Play and went to sit on the back steps to smoke a cigarette, because he was so close to losing it, it wasn't even funny.

They had company coming soon. Charlie had devolved from "a bad day" to "a bad week," Walter had started shitting in the bathtub, Noah was teething, Bruiser was losing his hair, and Beckett had to be in the office most every day.

He chased the end of the Marlboro with his lighter, his hands shaking so bad he couldn't hardly do it.

Bruiser started barking, which had to mean Beck just got home. How the fuck did it get to be so late in the day? He had beds to make and dinner, and he hadn't even showered yet today. Or yesterday. When was the last time he'd showered?

If Beck so much as blinked at him, he was going to get in his truck, find a bar, and get into a fight. Which, he wouldn't, but promising himself he could made him feel better.

He was out there alone for a bit, longer than he would have expected given Charlie's screaming and the chocolate milk everywhere. That sliding glass door finally opened, though, and he braced himself...just in case.

"Hey, Stud." Beck stepped in close, gently took his lighter from his fingers, and replaced it with an ice-cold beer. "Pizza will be here in forty-five."

"Thank you." His voice was trembling, and he hated that, but he was stupidly grateful for the kid gloves. He needed them right now.

Beck hooked an arm around his shoulders and gave him a little squeeze. "Nice evening, huh? You know how I love the way the sunset hits the mountains this time of year."

"Yeah, there's going to be snow any day, but this is good." He leaned in hard, sucking in comfort and warmth in equal amounts. "I'm sorry."

"Nothing to be sorry for. Charlie and I had a quick talk, and she and I are going to clean up the kitchen when she is ready. Noah is happy as a clam, playing in baby jail. You are unfortunately, only human. Not much you can do about that." Beck kissed his temple.

"I had to put her in her room, baby. I was so pissed off. I needed some time to cool down." It seemed like a shitty thing to do, but he'd been so fucking mad.

"I actually think that was a great idea. She's fine, and she knows you're mad. She got the point, and you almost got a cigarette." He heard the little tease in Beck's voice. "Win-almost-win?"

"You're not pissed at me?" The relief was crushing—that his classy lover thought he was doing okay, that he wasn't just some giant mean asshole that couldn't handle a three-year-old.

Beck turned and pulled him in, hugging him close. "Hey. I've got your back, baby. We have one job. Try to keep these kids alive until they turn eighteen. So far, so good."

"Right. Only eighteen years and a couple of months left to go. We can do this." Thank God for his Beck. He wanted so bad to be good at this whole dad thing, because his hadn't been, but he was scared that he was just...shit at it.

"With a little luck and a little wine, I think we've got this." Beck let him go and caught his eyes. "You give a shit. You love those kids."

"I do. I love them to death." And the beer was doing its part of the job of calming him the fuck down.

Beck shrugged. "What else do they need?"

The screen door opened as Charlie poked her head out. "Pappy, I'm quiet now."

Beck gave him a wink and turned to Charlie. "Okay. So you're ready to clean up your mess?"

"Uh-huh." She was pouting. If that lower lip stuck out any farther, he'd be able to balance his beer on it.

"Let's get it done then. Pizza is coming."

Charlie glanced up at Sky, looked away, then looked at him again.

He sat on the step, on her level and opened his arms. Apologies were important, respecting him was important, but love was the most important, full stop.

She ran right to him and hugged him. "You were *mad*, Papa."

"I was. That was very mean of you, and it hurt my feelings pretty bad."

She nodded and sniffled. "Sorry I hurt your feelings."

"Thank you." He hugged her tight. "I love you, Charlie-girl."

"I love you, Papa!" She kissed his cheek and patted his face. "Are you okay? Pappy said we need to let you breathe. Are you breathing?"

Beck chuckled and cleared his throat. "Come on baby, let's get this done."

"I'll come help so we're done by pizza." He squeezed Beck's hand. "What kind did you order, love?"

"I got a small plain one and a big veggie one for us." Noah stuck his arms up in the air as they came inside, and Beck scooped him up. "Hey, little man. Can you say 'pizza'?"

"Pee-sa!" Noah could say it, and he knew what it was too.

"I texted Lacey to see if she could come by tomorrow. We need a more realistic plan. You're going to lose your mind trying to get your invitational set up while home alone with these two." Beck brought Noah into the kitchen and sat him in his chair.

"Oh." He nodded, his emotions swinging wildly between shame that he hadn't been enough and crushing relief that Beck understood what he needed. "I love being here with them, but we need a nanny. We need help, especially once the new baby comes."

"We need a nanny. And Lacey loves them. I think we should hire her. Period. Full-time." He handed out damp rags, and Beck pulled out the stepladder. "I got the ceiling."

"Sister, you work on the cabinets wiping them off." He started on the floor. "I agree. I think she's a great person, a great nanny, and she loves the kids."

"And you should work with her on what schedule you

need, you know? So we can work when we need to and be more…relaxed with the kids when we're not." Beck was going to have to keep a pretty regular schedule, Sky knew that, and some days were longer than others. It wasn't like they couldn't afford some help.

"Right. That should be easy to figure out." And he felt his shoulders come down from his ears. "Are you going to be able to be here to meet with her too?"

"Sure. I'll be anywhere you want me, Stud." Beck climbed off the ladder and peered up at the ceiling. "I think I got it all. How'd you do on the cabinets, girlie?"

"Good! No more sticky."

"Good girl. No more throwing drinks, okay? If you want to talk, we'll chat." He winked at her, trying to straddle the line between firm and not ramping things up.

"Okay." She handed him her gross rag. Charlie was three. This wouldn't be her last temper tantrum. But maybe she'd make less of a mess next time.

"I think we should work on the office while my folks are here too. They'll entertain each other. If I can get comfortable in there, I might work from home sometimes." They hadn't even touched the office yet.

"Sounds like a great idea. Do you feel comfortable keeping it up here in the formal living room, or do you want to be downstairs with more privacy? We could hang a door on the living room, even." He wanted them all to be able to spend time together but be comfortable too.

"We need the guest room downstairs, so let's keep it up here. You'll be in there more than I will. You want a door? It would make phone calls easier, for sure. Let's do it."

Noah fussed a little, and Beck stuck a handful of Cheerios on his tray without blinking an eye. "You feel better? You look better. This has been a rough week, I know."

"I do. Thank you. You helped more than I can say." He met Beck's eyes, and his smile was real this time. "I love you."

"It was probably the beer." Beck smiled back. "I love you too."

10

Beckett held the office door steady while Sky dropped the screws into the new frame they'd installed that morning. Man, they'd been working hard for two days. The office had a fresh coat of paint. They'd rearranged the furniture and figured out their tech issues. Dad had pitched in and cleaned the fireplace and repainted the mantel for them.

And they hadn't seen much of the kids in the last two days either. Mom was in heaven.

They'd all earned a day of football and food coma tomorrow.

He looked over at Sky, who was hot as hell with that power drill in his hands. "Getting close, huh?"

"We are. This is going to work out nicely for privacy and access both." Sky dropped his voice to a whisper. "Your dad hasn't pretended to not hear me this whole trip."

"I noticed that." He wasn't sure what it meant, but he was happy for Sky. Sky hadn't had a good dad experience, and Beck had always wanted them to get along. He and Sky had talked about it on and off over the years, and neither of them had ever figured out what Dad's hang-up was. "Maybe he's finally decided you're real."

Dad liked being useful and having a project; maybe he was just in a good mood.

"Maybe. Bubba there sure likes him. It's adorable." Noah had been latched on to Dad from the start.

"You think it's the beard? Or maybe the deep voice." Dad's voice was so deep he practically rumbled when he talked.

He stepped back and had a look, opening and closing the door a couple of times. "Just have to put the knobs on. Nice work, Stud." He'd had no idea how to hang a door, but Sky had installed the frame and everything without scratching his head once.

"Thank you, thank you!" Sky bowed. "I am useful as well as decorative."

"Papa! She says she'll be my granny. Is that okay?" Charlie ran up, and then she blinked. "Papa. You made a door."

"I did. And I think that's amazing. You get a granny and a grampa. How cool!"

His mom came walking up behind her. "She seemed pleased."

"Oh, I'm sure she isn't the only one who's happy, Mom."

"No. No, you're right about that." Mom touched his shoulder and smiled at him. "Look at the door. You're a wonder, Skyler."

"Hey, I helped!" Beckett rolled his eyes.

"My Papa is a cowboy," Charlie said, with that gravity peculiar to three going on four. "He can make a whole door."

"He is a cowboy. My grandfather was too. They're good to have around." Mom gave Sky the same shoulder pat she'd just given him. "Are you hungry, guys? I was going to make your dad a sandwich."

He nodded. He wasn't starving, but he liked the idea of Mom making him a sandwich. It was weird but true. "I could definitely eat. Sky?"

"I would never turn down a sandwich, ma'am. Thank you."

"What's a ma'am, Papa?"

"Well, let me explain..." Sky led Charlie away, talking hard in that straightforward way that seemed to be a language their eldest got.

"He's good with her, isn't he?" Mom ran her hand over the door, clearly impressed, and headed for the kitchen.

He trailed along after her and went to the sink to wash up. "He's amazing. I couldn't do this without him."

"Oh, I think you could. But I'm glad that you don't have to." Mom handed him a towel to dry his hands. "I love that she says she's a cowboy."

"Sky taught her that. People like to try to argue with her, but she won't have it. Papa says she can be a cowboy and that's that."

"He's so...basic is the wrong word...no-nonsense. He appeals to her need for simple order." Dad walked in, Noah on his hip. "You're infinitely more complicated and complex, but he's just a simple man with a straightforward view of the world."

So...was that a compliment or an insult? Was it just a fact?

Beck knew how he felt about it. "He's exactly what I need. I tend to make things way more complicated than they need to be. He doesn't let me think myself into an ulcer."

"Which you got from your father." Mom's little dig at Dad made him grin.

Dad sighed and bounced Noah, playfully. "You tell your grandmother to be nice to me, Noah."

"Turkey or ham, Beckett?"

"Can I have a little of both, please?"

Mom rolled her eyes. "Of course. Strange child. And Skyler?"

"He'll eat anything you put in front of him, I promise." Sky was easy that way.

"Turkey, then, for him and your father." Mom nodded, and that settled that.

"Me too! Pappy! Me too, her!"

That was pretty clear, really. "Noah would like a half sandwich, please, Granny."

"How about Charlotte?" His mom was bustling around, pulling things from the fridge and setting them on the counter.

"Charlie likes roll-ups. Turkey with cheese is her favorite. Let me help, Mom." He pulled out the bread and some paper plates.

"Shoo, you. I can still feed my family, thank you." She grinned and kissed his cheek. "Go show your father the new car. He's dying to drive it."

Go show your father the car? That was a guy-talk thing. Did his mom think they needed to talk? Did Dad want to talk? He looked at Dad and shrugged. "Want to see it? The dashboard reminds me of an airplane or something."

"I do. Should I put him…"

Noah's eyes lit up. "Go bye-bye?"

"No, Noah, we're going to just look at the car."

"Go bye-bye."

Sky appeared with Charlie. "Bubba! Dude, want to go outside and play trucks with Sister before lunch?"

"Trucks, Sis'r!"

"Get y'all's coats and tell Bruiser." Sky winked at him on the way through the kitchen.

"Bruiser! We're going outside!" Charlie hollered. "Walter! You want to come too?"

Walter didn't even pick his head up to look at her. He reached up to the perch at the top of the cat tree and gave Walter a scritch. "He's gonna nap, girlie."

"Okay, bye, Walter!"

He tossed his dad's coat over and pulled his on before heading out to the garage. "So, you really want to see the car? Or am I in trouble?"

"I really want to see the car, and I really want to make sure you're okay. You went from no kids to two kids to three kids soon. Your mother and I are worried. We're talking about moving closer, so we can help, be involved." Dad looked at him, so seriously. "I was worried about Skyler. He's not the person I would have chosen to be with you, but you can see the love he has—for you and the children. It's not for show. That's special."

Wow. That was a lot of words for his dad. And a lot to talk about. He wasn't sure where to start.

"We were incredibly overwhelmed at first, yeah. Connor was a friend so there was that, and then these two little ones...but we've got good friends and a good community. We have a great nanny. I have paternity leave for the new baby." He squinted at his father, trying to get a read on him. "You want to move up here? Really? Or is Mom panicking?"

"We want to downsize. We're thinking of a condo. Something easy. If we're going to have to move anyway..."

Dad had always liked it up here. He visited a couple of times a year, and they'd go out on the boat or go fishing, so that part wasn't a shock. But moving up here to be near him, and— "Sky lives here, you know."

"I am aware of that." Dad shot him a look—the one that pinned him to the wall as a little boy. "He hurt you, badly, and I don't think he's good enough for you. But he is making up for leaving you."

He wasn't a little boy anymore, though.

"We hurt each other, as it turns out. Yeah, maybe he left, but I'm the one that told him not to come back. And...no, you know what?" He took a deep breath and kept his temper in check. "If you can't respect him, if you can't treat him like a son, then please don't move here. He's my best friend, my husband, he's an amazing dad....I'd literally be lost without him right now. There's no one in the world who could be better for me."

His father looked at him, and a slow smile bloomed across his face. "Good. Good for you. We all deserve to be that much in love with our spouse. All of us."

His eyebrow shot up so hard it almost hurt, and Beck stared at his father like he'd never seen the man before. "We do. And I am. I just want you to see him like I do. You need to look harder. Okay?"

"Fair enough." Dad nodded to the car. "Show me this fancy thing."

Conversation over, apparently.

"You got it. Get in." He opened the driver's side door. Score one for Mom.

He couldn't wait to talk to Sky.

He did like their SUV. It had all the bells and whistles, so, as Sky told him, it could be a family car and also a date car. He showed his dad the gadgets and buttons, the satellite radio and the navigation screen, and promised they could go for a drive later.

"Pappy, Granny says come get your lunch!"

"How did you end up with her calling you Pappy?" Dad asked, and he chuckled, shaking his head.

"Well, 'Dad' or 'Daddy' seemed tacky, and she picked it. It took Noah just a few days."

"Pappy! Hurry!"

"Coming, sweetie! We better hurry, Gramps. You don't want to see her mad." He winked and got out of the car.

"No, no. I don't want to see that." Dad laughed and followed him back into the house, stopping him outside the kitchen. "Hey. I'm sorry about your friend."

He nodded. "Thanks, Dad."

"Sammich!" Noah sang, holding it out for him to see.

He smiled at his boy and kissed his head. "Sammich! Is it good, buddy?"

"Granny made me roll-ups, Pappy. Just like you do."

He gave Charlotte a hug. "Aren't you the luckiest?"

"Uh-huh. Papa says Santa Claus comes Thursday. The *real* Santa. He's on the TV. Did you know that?"

He grinned. "The real one? Well, if Papa says so, then it must be true, right?" He stepped up behind Sky and hugged his husband to his chest. "I can't wait."

"Me either." Sky leaned into him, laughing softly. "I wonder if Granny and Grampa can babysit one day this weekend for s-h-o-p-p-i-n-g."

God, he loved Sky's laugh. He loved all his family in one room. He loved the way he caught Dad watching them out of the corner of his eye.

He'd never imagined for a minute this would be his amazing life.

"Yes. We can babysit. We would love to." Mom to the rescue.

"*Excelente, mamita.* I appreciate it." Sky blew Mom a kiss. "Maybe Saturday. Black Friday is he-horrible."

"We'll all be moving too slowly on Friday anyway. Especially Dad." Mom smiled at his father. "He'll be worn out from sitting on his rump watching football."

"Exhausted. I'm an old man, you know." Dad looked at Sky. Like, right at him. Right in the eye. "Skyler, are you making those sausage balls again? I do look forward to them."

"I am, sir. It's not Thanksgiving without sausage balls." Sky grinned wide. "I'm glad y'all could come. I wanted the kids to have some grandparent time with both y'all before the new baby comes."

Beck debated whether to tell Sky they were thinking about moving right now or to wait until he could have the full conversation he wanted to and let Sky have a second to sit with it. He decided to wait.

"We live for grandparent time. It's important for children to know their grandparents."

Do not ask about his parents. Don't ask, Dad. Don't—

"Are your folks still in Texas, Skyler?"

Damn. That was Mom. Hadn't he told her this story already?

"I assume so, ma'am. Come eat your sandwich, Pappy. Charlie and Bubba have almost finished theirs." Sky winked at Mom, effectively shutting her up.

"I'm starved. Did you finish yours already?" He grabbed his plate and a stool by the island and dug in.

Mom didn't ask anything else. She did reach over and give Sky's hand a squeeze, though.

"Is this one mine, honey? Is there mayo on it?" Dad picked right up on it and effectively finished shifting the conversation.

"There is." Mom looked so sad, but Sky was better off. Sky deserved to be loved, not reviled.

"I think we should all play cards tonight," Sky offered. "I hear y'all have started playing Spades."

Mom lit up. "Do you know how?"

"Yes, ma'am. I love to play cards." His Sky was trying hard.

"I think that's a great idea. Mom and I would like nothing better than to kick our sons' behinds at Spades." Dad looked between them. "Both of them."

Sky's eyes twinkled at Dad, and Beck was so proud. So incredibly proud. "We'll see about that. Say if we win, Mom makes those cinnamon rolls for breakfast tomorrow?"

"You're on, cowboy." Mom rubbed her hands together. She would make them anyway, he knew. Just because Sky liked them.

Dad crossed his arms. "And if we win?"

"Charlie will make you scrambled eggs." Beck grinned.

"I'm good at that! Right, Papa?"

"You are amazing at that, Charlie-girl. I love your eggs."

"You can make eggs, Charlie?" Mom went wide-eyed.

"Uh-huh."

"Yes, ma'am," Sky whispered, and she nodded.

"Yes, ma'am. I can make eggs!"

And that was that. They were having scrambled eggs and cinnamon rolls for breakfast. It didn't matter who actually won, it was more about how the game was played.

Finally, it felt like his parents and Sky got that too.

11

"Papa."

"Papa?"

Sky opened his eyes; then he saw Charlie standing there. "What's up, Charlie-girl?"

"I want my daddy. Can I come sleep with you?"

He nodded and opened his arms. She'd been riled up, and today was Thanksgiving. She had new fathers, new grandparents, and everyone was excited. "Come on up, honey."

She crawled up, and he cuddled her in, pulling the blankets up over their heads. "I love you, Papa."

"I love you, Charlie. So much. Are you excited about Thanksgiving?"

"I'm excited about cimminom rolls."

"Oh, me too."

She tapped his chin. "What does Thanksgiving mean?"

"Do you know about being thankful?"

She shook her head.

"Thankful is when things are good, when people make things better—there's a feeling in your heart that says, 'That was good.' That's thankful." He grinned at her, hoping he was getting through. He thought he could, because he knew all about being thankful. He was a lucky bastard, and he gave thanks most every day. "Thanksgiving is where you have good food and think about that feeling in your heart. Like I'm thankful for you and Bubba and Pappy and Granny and Grampa."

"What about Bruiser and Walter and Violet and Apple?"

She got it. She so got it. "And Apple and Violet and Walter and Bruiser. Absolutely."

"I'm thankful for Walter even if he doesn't know I love him yet." She was so determined. "He will."

"Yes, ma'am. He will. He just needs to figure out how." Maybe. Maybe Walter would just glare at her until she was grown. He didn't know.

Charlie yawned wide and settled hard against him. "I will be thankful tomorrow. I'm sleepy."

Beckett chuckled low and soft. But didn't interrupt.

"Sounds perfect, angel girl. I love you."

"I love you, Papa. So much. Pappy too."

He kissed the top of her head, giving thanks for his baby girl and his baby boy and his upcoming little one.

"Good night, sweetie," Beck whispered. She muttered something back but was already almost asleep.

"Is she okay?"

"Just a lot of stuff going on, I think—she needed us."

"She needed her cowboy. I get it." Beck rolled over to face him. "It is a lot, though. She's right about that."

"Yeah. It is. Your mom wants to move here, did she tell you? I bet your sister is fixin' to swallow her tongue."

"Oh, she told you? Dad told me while I was showing him the car. Allison's boys are older, I guess. And Dad hates

Southern California." Beck sighed. "So...what do you think?"

"I think that you and me have a life. I think that our world used to be one thing and now it's another thing." His family was gone or far away—his biological family, his cowboy family, and they would need help to raise these babies. Beck's people loved Beckett, and they were gonna love these babies.

"Do you want that other thing to include my parents being around? Dad was definitely feeling me out."

"They're not bad people. If they want to be grandparents, isn't that good?"

"I think so." Beck rested a warm hand on his cheek. "And you should know...Dad and I had a talk. I made sure he understood how important you are to me. And to the kids."

"Thank you. I don't want to be at odds with your people. I love you, I love our babies, our pets, our home—I'm all in. Have been."

"I know. He...just needed to see you like I do. He's going to be great. I really think so." Beck kissed him gently and smiled, he could just make it out in the dark. "You know what today is? Eight weeks to baby."

"Is that all? I can't believe it. I want to meet this little one so bad." He'd moved from terrified to feeling like he loved this whole being a daddy thing with his entire being.

"Me too. I'm so impatient. And I know we can do this. With Mom and Dad and Lacey...our friends. We're lucky. These kids have a village. My little baby Sky." Beck had turned a corner too; he didn't seem to worry every minute, was more in the moment.

"And our Charlie and Noah. We've got one good-sized family."

"We do. All of a sudden." Beck nodded. "I know it's not

what you...you're an amazing father, Sky. Thank you for being in this with me."

"I never thought I'd—" Sky sighed softly. "Gay cowboys don't get happily ever afters. They just don't."

"I intend to make sure that you do, Stud. That's my job." Beck tapped his chest. "This gay cowboy is getting a happy ever after and then some. I promise."

"I'm a lucky man. We got this—you and me. Thanksgiving, Christmas, New Year's, and new baby." Christ, they needed a calendar just for birthdays.

"Not a baby. A *dragon*." Charlie mumbled. "A dragon."

"A dragon?" Just what they needed. A dragon of their own.

"The costume," Beck whispered. "They'll be a baby dressed like a dragon, sweetie."

"The baby can stay a dragon." Charlie seemed very sure about this.

Beck laughed softly. "You want a dragon for a baby brother or sister?"

Charlie sighed, frustrated with Beck. "I don't *need* a brother or sister. I already *have* one."

"You don't have a sister, Charlie-girl, but everyone needs a dragon." Although they did have Walter...

She lifted her head and peered at him, and he swore for a second she seemed older than three. "Yes. A dragon." She lay back down again. "Daddy's going to miss Santa."

He wasn't going to cry. He wasn't, dammit. "Yeah, but I swear to God, Santa will not miss you, and neither will your papa and your pappy."

Beck found his free hand and held on tight. "Hey, Charlie? Do you know how important you are? You and Noah?"

"Important?"

"Mhm. You two made us a family. That's an amazing thing. There will always be people we're going to miss. But we have each other now, and that's important."

"I love you too, Pappy." She snuggled in with a sigh. "Today is good. Granny is coming to see us again."

Beckett kissed her head. "She is. And she is going to make mashed potatoes and pumpkin pie. My two favorite Thanksgiving foods. You can help her, and you can watch the parade and then football with us, if you want to."

"Do I like football, Papa?"

"I don't know. There's lots of cheering and stuff. That's pretty cool. You'll have to try it out." He wasn't a huge follower of who was playing who, but he knew the rules, and he liked the games, as a rule. Especially college ball.

"Your grampa loves football. I like to watch it with him because he makes it fun. You should try it out. But..." Beck fussed with the covers, pretending to get her tucked in. "Right now, you should go to sleep. You can stay with us if you want to, but it'll be morning soon and we don't want to be sleepy on Thanksgiving, do we?"

"No, Pappy. I want to be thanky."

Sky fought his laughter with all he was.

Beck grinned at him and looked back at Charlie. "We are going to be *so* thanky." Beck kissed her again. "Close your eyes, girlie. Sleep well."

" 'Kay, Pappy. You too, Papa. Pappy says so. No talking."

Beck's stifled laugh sounded like a strangled duck. "Good night, Papa."

"Good night, Pappy." *Asshole. Beautiful fucking asshole.*

12

"Dad traced his hand on a piece of paper and he and Charlie are coloring it and turning it into a turkey." Beck wandered into the kitchen for another cup of coffee and stopped short in the middle of the room. "Mom. Your pie smells so good."

"Thank you, kiddo. We used to do that with you. We even made Thanksgiving place mats out of them one year. Don't you remember?" Mom had on an apron she must have packed and brought with her just for this occasion. That was so...Mom.

"Kind of? I remember using the place mats for a couple of years anyway."

"Well, you made them. You and your sister. You were about...eight. Ali was six, I guess. Such a long time ago now."

"Is Dad okay?"

Mom looked at him. "What do you mean?"

"I don't know. He's different." Sitting on the floor and making turkey drawings with Charlie, accepting Sky, wanting to move up north again. Giving Sky a run for his money at Spades.

"He is. Isn't it wonderful? He's happiest when he has something to do, as you know. When he feels useful. He loves that you boys are including him in the work on the house and trusting him with Noah and Charlie."

"Huh." He poured himself a fresh cup of coffee and added a little creamer. "Why wouldn't we trust him?"

"Oh, it's not that. It's just that Ali is a very...particular parent. And Gary doesn't let anyone near his tools."

Beck laughed. "There is always something to be done around this house. Sky and I have a project nearly every weekend." And now, with the kids and the new baby coming, they'd really have trouble keeping up.

"Well, that's it. Sky let him help, listened to him. Those kids need extended family and opened up to him." She put the marshmallows on top of the casserole. "He's bored. Retirement isn't fun if no one lets him do things. You boys have work. Sky has to travel sometimes, you need to be in court sometimes, and nannies need days off. We want to be a part of things, and..." She shrugged and winked at him. "And there's a new baby coming. Three under three is a challenge for the most experienced parents."

" 'Three under three' is a thing? When you say it like that, it makes me feel incredibly unprepared." Who was he kidding? They *were* incredibly unprepared. "And tired."

"Yeah. If it's okay, we'd like to come out after the baby is born. We're talking about renting a condo and seeing if we like condo life. Your sister wants to buy our house."

Of course she did.

"She lives in SoCal but wants to buy your house in Florida." He deadpanned. "Mom, I love her, but what the hell?"

"Tsk. Language, please."

"Okay. What the ever-loving heck?" He grinned.

"It's your sister, dear. You know she's panicking about the idea of us moving. She doesn't love change."

"I'll call her next week when you've gone home, and we'll talk it out. I think it's good that you're coming here. We appreciate it." They needed the help now, and Mom and Dad would need their help sometimes too. It would be good to have them close. He'd always assumed they'd go to California, so it was still such a surprise that they'd chosen to come here. "Do you want to ride around on Sunday and see some places? I'll drive."

"I'd love that. And I'll need you to get me the name of your realtor at some point, but there's no hurry. Come put this in the oven for me, please? We have cheese and crackers for nibbles. I wasn't sure if it was safe from Walter on the table."

He took the dish and set it in the oven for her. "Nothing is safe from Walter if he's determined. He's not that interested in cheese. Wait until the turkey is done, though, he'll be underfoot."

"I need to let Sky know I'm done so he can make his sausage balls."

"He went out to bring up some wood. You go sit with the kids, Mom. I'll get him." His stubborn cowboy insisted on doing it even though it was more of a chore for him than most. This would be a great excuse to go help without looking like that was why he was there.

Beck got Mom settled with a cup of tea and ducked out the sliding glass door onto the deck.

"Hey, babe. It's still snowing, Charlie's making hand-turkeys, and Noah is either singing, learning to yodel, or signaling aliens. I'm not quite sure which." Sky grinned at him, giving him what he thought of as the Sky report.

"Ah, yes. I have seen the hand-turkeys for myself, but no aliens yet." And the snow was light, but it was supposed to go on for a while. "I'll grab an armload and finish piling the wood up. Mom says the kitchen is all yours. Her pie is in the oven. And did I hear there was a kiss for your husband in the forecast?"

"I think you might have heard right, husband of mine." Sky beamed at him, then caught him around the waist and took a happy kiss.

Beck inhaled, getting a little of that hardworking cowboy scent. "You did great out here. Thank you."

"Love you, babe. More than is reasonable." Sky rested their foreheads together.

The slider opened, and Dad's deep voice interrupted them. "Um. Gentlemen? Sorry to interrupt but, uh, Mom is reading with Charlie, and Noah has had a bit of a blowout..."

Sky cracked up. "Yay! Blowouts!" He rolled his eyes and grinned. "You want me to finish this, make sausage balls, or clean a boy that is going to get potty trained or else?"

"Help Dad clean the boy, I'll finish this, and then I'll help you with your balls." He waggled his eyebrows at Sky.

"Coward." Sky headed in with a grin, already teasing Noah good-naturedly, playing with their son.

"Yup," he muttered as Sky went inside. But there was nothing bad about Sky and Dad bonding over baby stuff.

By the time he'd finished with the wood, trudged around to the mudroom and pulled off his snowy clothes, Dad and Sky were in the kitchen. Dad had Noah on his hip and was watching Sky work.

"But Laura grew up on a farm. Her grandparents had a ranch. I should have known I was being taken for a ride when she made the bet. She outshot me four to one."

He remembered that story. Dad had made some flip comment about men having steadier hands than women, and she'd challenged him to an afternoon at the shooting range. Dad didn't know then that her grandfather had given her a rifle for her tenth birthday.

Dad shook his head and patiently removed Noah's fingers from his nose. "Anyway, I learned my lesson."

"There are some people you just don't bet against. Now I know, don't bet against Mom."

"Papa. Gampa. Papa. Gampa. Papa. Gampa. *Pappy!*" The little song was pure joy, his little boy filled with happiness.

"Hey, buddy." He smiled at Noah and kissed him on the forehead. "You want me to take him, Dad?"

"I've got him. We have a little dance going." Dad bounced Noah in a circle.

"Offer stands." Beck pulled up a stool at the island. "I swear, I have never seen a happier baby. He is almost never grumpy."

"He has two fathers that adore him, and a grampa that thinks he's amazing!" God, Dad was cute.

"How's the sausage coming, Stud?" The house smelled so good already, and dinner wasn't for hours yet.

"It's good. I'll slide them in two batches into the toaster oven. They'll be great."

"Grandma is helping me make a list for Santa!" Charlie came running in with a piece of paper in her hand and put it on the counter.

"Oh, yeah?" Man, his mom was good at this shit. "Let me see."

Charlie turned it over and eyeballed him. "It's for *Santa*, Pappy."

"Ohhh." He hid his grin. "Sorry."

"You'll need to write one for Noah too, Charlie-girl." Sky winked at her. "Sausage balls are in the oven."

"I can write one for him. He wants a toy truck, a rocking horse, and a ball."

"A rocking horse is a great idea." Mom started writing on the back side of Charlie's list. "A truck...and a ball. Santa is going to be very well prepared. I'm going to put this on the refrigerator, sweetheart. Then your dads can help you add to it as you think of things."

"Thanks, Mom." Their shopping trip would be much better now.

"Thank you, Granny!" Charlie ran to Mom, hugged her tight. "Papa, Santa can find me here, right?"

"Yes. Santa so can." There was zero doubt in Sky's voice. "I promise."

"Santa knows everything. He knows where you are already," Dad said, borrowing Sky's certainty. "He found me in the army, he can find you here at home. Don't you worry."

"Everyone move aside, please. I need to get my pie out of the oven."

Beck scooped Charlie up and moved out of Mom's way. "I am so ready to eat this meal. I've been a good boy for days."

"Pappy, you have to be a good boy. Papa's got hims eyes on you."

His mother set her pie down on the counter and turned her back, but he could see her shoulders shaking. *Damn her.* And Dad left the kitchen with Noah entirely because he couldn't hold his laughter in at all.

He didn't dare look at Sky.

Beck looked at Charlie with wide eyes. "Papa sees everything."

"Uh-huh. Papa is magic." She looked at him, so serious, so firm.

Sky didn't so much as crack a smile.

"He is. He is magic." Beck had no argument with that at all. Everything about his cowboy was magic.

A timer went off.

"Oh, I think that's the turkey! Shall we check it?" Mom grabbed some oven mitts. "Come on, Skyler, you grab the thermometer and let's see."

"Coming! Charlie-girl, you stay back, this is hot." Sky looked so completely happy, just at peace with the world for right this second.

"Charlie's with me, baby." Beck was never going to get tired of seeing Sky hanging out with his parents, spending all this time. He wouldn't force it, but he really hoped that having them close would give Sky something he might be missing.

"Okay, I'll pull it out a little, and you let me know if she's done."

Mom laughed at something Sky said, and it was Thanksgiving—not just the food, but the whole package.

"Come on, Charlie. Let's go set the table." He led her out of the kitchen as the turkey came out of the oven. There would be all kinds of bustling around now, and it was better they not be underfoot.

The tablecloth was already out, so he handed Charlie a stack of forks to put at each place.

"No fork for Bubba. He gets a little one," Charlie reminded him.

"You're right about that." He helped her set them out and he found knives and serving utensils. "So." He looked at his dad. "Mom says you guys are ready for a little drive on Sunday to see some places. We're excited."

"Are you?" At his nod, Dad relaxed and smiled. "Good deal. We're planning to rent a condo for six months, sell the house, then buy."

Charlie looked at Dad. "What's that mean?"

"It means your granny and I want to live close and visit a lot."

"Oh. Okay."

"We're really grateful for the help. And the more family around the better." Beck ruffled Charlie's hair. "Grab the napkins off that chair for me, girlie?"

"Yes, sir!"

Dad chuckled. "You're raising cowboys."

"I seem to be. It makes Sky happy, and if he's happy, I'm happy. We could do worse than having polite kids, right?" He'd fallen for a cowboy after all, why not raise them too?

"I think it's adorable. I can't wait to meet the new baby. Sky is sure it's a little girl. What do you think?"

"I think I'm going to love it to bits, whatever it is. It's Sky's, you know? But I'm going with his theory. His dreams tend to be weirdly accurate." Sky seemed so sure that it made him sure. He'd be surprised if it was a boy at this point. Just as happy either way, but surprised.

"It's a dragon!" Charlie stomped her little foot. "I told you."

Beck winked at his dad. "Charlie has picked out a dragon costume for the baby to wear home from the hospital."

"Oh. I think a dragon baby would be very interesting. Maybe we should go shopping together and get you a dragon stuffie to love on."

Charlie's eyes went wide. "We can do that?"

"Sure we can. Granny and I are babysitting on Saturday, so I think you and I could have an adventure."

Wow. Dad had this grandparenting thing down.

"Pappy? I can go? Please?" Look at those huge, green eyes, lit up and pleading.

Beck smiled at her. "Of course. It sounds like fun."

"And no Noah."

"Nope, just you me and a stuffed dragon."

"Papa!" Charlie ran toward the kitchen. "Papa! Grampa's going to take me to...*ooh*."

Beck laughed. "Sounds like dinner is ready. Come on, Dad."

The table was groaning under the weight of food, and Mom and Sky looked incredibly pleased with themselves.

"Papa...that's lots."

Sky chuckled softly. "Your granny did an amazing job."

"Oh, stop. It's your Papa's table; he did most of the work." Mom gave Sky a kiss on the cheek. "Charmer. Who carves? You or Beckett?"

"Beckett does a better job, Mom." Sky looked at him, eyes shimmering gently.

"Are you thanky, Papa?"

"Oh, baby girl. I am the most thanky papa on earth."

What Beck wanted to do was grab his husband up and kiss that thanky face. But for now, he returned Sky's look with a knowing smile and mouthed, *I love you.*

He picked up the carving set. He didn't really do a better job, but he enjoyed carving the turkey, and Sky knew it. He set to work, removing the big wings and drumsticks first.

Bruiser was close by, partly because everyone else was here, so of course he had to keep an eye on things, but mostly because he wanted a bite. "Good boy," he said and put a couple of little chunks of dark meat on a plate.

"Charlie, will you take that into the kitchen for Bruiser? Just put the plate on the floor, sweetie."

"Uh-huh. And Walter too. Walter is thanky." Charlie took the plate. "Come on, Bruiser! Have thanky turkey!"

"I'd correct her," Mom said. "But it's the cutest thing ever."

"I have no intention of correcting her." He laughed, carving happily. "This is cooked perfectly, you guys. I can't wait to dig in. Go on and sit, Mom, Dad. Start the potatoes going around."

Dad pulled out Mom's chair for her, then tucked Noah into his seat. Noah had been watching everything like always. Such a quiet baby but smart. He could see it. "What can he eat, Skyler?"

"Anything he wants. He loves sausage balls. I fed him one earlier." Sky waggled his eyebrows. "He is also a huge fan of guacamole."

Dad laughed and started cutting up little bites for Noah. "Who isn't a fan of guacamole?"

Beck served up the sliced turkey on a big platter and took the carcass back to the kitchen, where he snuck Walter a couple of little bites before returning to his seat.

"I know Sky will want to say something in a minute, but first, I just want to say that if anyone had told me last Thanksgiving what this Thanksgiving was going to look like I'd have laughed at them. Seriously. I'm usually a planner, and Sky is so organized and prepared. And man, we were not ready for all of this. We have friends and family to be grateful for, for sure. So, thanks for being here, Mom and Dad."

"We wouldn't dream of being anywhere else." And he believed that from his father. He believed it with all his heart.

Sky picked Charlie up and nodded. "Charlie and me, we'd like to say grace, so if y'all would bow your heads. Okay, Charlie-girl. We're fixin' to give thanks, like we practiced."

"Dear God. Bless the turkey and Bubba and Dragon Baby. Papa and Pappy and Granny and Grampa. Bless Bruiser and Walter. Tell Momma and Daddy in Heaven I love them." Charlie glanced at Sky. "That's good?"

"That's perfect. Bless this family and this food. In Jesus's name. Amen."

"Amen. That was really nice, Charlie. Thank you." Beck reached over and gave her hand a squeeze, then let his fingers brush over Sky's arm as he sat down again. "Is it me, or does the turkey seem like the least important thing on this table?"

"I could be happy with the sausage balls and some of Mom's pie," Dad teased.

"Really. I could just have a plate of mashed potatoes and some gravy and call it a day." He grinned. He wouldn't, but he could.

"I want a little bit of everything." Sky took a spoonful of all the dishes, testing every little bit. It was sweet, and he could tell it meant something to Mom, because she beamed across the table.

He followed suit and ended up with a huge plate that he knew he'd never get through. He made a good run at it, though. He noticed that Noah did too, feeding himself bites of turkey and trying so hard to get the mashed potatoes on his spoon.

He finally leaned back in his head with a sigh. "How is it, Mom?"

"Wonderful." She winked at him. "The food is excellent too."

"Granny, can you teach Pappy how to make *these* tatoes? Please?"

"Well, I can try." Mom shook her head. "Pappy's going to need your help, though."

"These are better than mine, huh?"

Charlie nodded, and he had to agree. They were his favorite thing ever.

"Your granny makes the best mashed potatoes. They're amazing."

Sky and Dad both nodded, and Mom just looked tickled and a little teary.

"Okay, Dad. This is where we come in. Mom and Sky get to play with kids, and we get to clear the table and do the dishes." Beck eyed his father. "Have you digested enough to get up yet?"

"I'm not sure that's possible, but I'm game."

"You want to go outside and play, Charlie-girl? Or watch a cartoon and play Candy Land?" Sky stood and stretched, looking so full.

Charlie yawned, and he figured that was Sky's answer. "Cartoons?"

Beck started to mention that *The Wizard of Oz* was on at eight, but Charlie would probably be asleep by then. He thought maybe he'd run it by Dad instead, but Dad was tired, and by the time they were done with the dishes, he was making noises about going back to the B and B.

"This was a lovely, lovely day, boys. Thank you so much for having us." Mom gave out kisses, one for each of their cheeks.

"Thank you for all the cooking. Dinner was amazing." He and Sky followed them out to their car. Mom and Dad had bundled up, but he and Sky both shivered in the driveway.

"We'll see you tomorrow, y'all. We got no plans beyond leftovers and sleeping and watching the Wizard of Oz with Charlie. It'll be her first time." Sky looked so proud of himself. "I DVRed it, so Beck has to watch all the toy commercials with us."

He groaned. "Really?"

"Good night!" Mom closed the door, and Dad slowly pulled out of the driveway.

He looked at Sky. "Mom is saying, 'Watch out for deer, Tom.' " He got his arms around Sky and hustled him back toward the house.

"Lord have mercy, that was some good food. I may never eat again."

Ah, the eternal cry of...well, everyone after Thanksgiving.

"Until tomorrow." He turned off the living room lights and lifted Noah out of baby jail. "Come on, Charlie. Bedtime."

"Already, Pappy?"

Sky scooped her up. "Yep. Want to read the Grinch book, baby?"

"Uh-huh."

Noah frowned. "Me book!"

"You too! We can read the Grinch in the big bed. Want to?" The Grinch took on a whole new life with a Texas accent.

"Nightgown first. Then the big bed."

"Sounds great to me. What do you think, Papa?"

"Sounds perfect. I will grab the book and my jammies." Sky kissed Charlie's cheek. "Meet you in the big bed, m'dear."

"I'll get Noah changed." Beckett thought Sky looked so good. Happy, sleepy, even moving pretty well for having been on his feet all day. "Hey. I'm pretty damn thanky for you, Papa."

"Yeah? That's good, because I thank God for you every day."

Every day. And this had been a good one.

13

"Papa! Turn on the tree!"

"Papa! Turn on the lights, please?"

"Papa, Bubba wants to watch Santa!"

Sky chuckled softly and shook his head. Beckett was working late tonight, but they had a rhythm going and, to be honest, he was looking forward to supper together as adults, so it was chicken noodle soup and grilled cheese for the kiddos, baths, and *Santa Claus is Coming to Town* for the win.

The kids were utterly fascinated by the tree, and they'd made sure to incorporate the decorations from Connor, so that they'd have that to remember.

He'd spent an entire weekend decorating the outside well enough that someone could see their house from space, which tickled the hell out of the kids.

"Finish your soup, Charlie-girl. Then I'll get y'all in the tub, and then we will watch cartoons."

"I'm full," she whined, and puffed out her cheeks to prove it.

"Three more bites?" He remembered asking his mother

if he was going to have to take thirty more bites when he was grown.

"Three!" Noah repeated, happily stuffing his face with bites of grilled cheese.

"Ah, my hollow-legged boy." He chuckled and shook his head. "Your bubba knows how to chow down, *chica*."

Charlie slid her soup over toward Noah, and Sky calmly slid it right back.

She sighed. "Fine. Three more bites..." Charlie stuck her spoon into her soup and took three of the tiniest spoonfuls imaginable, then set her spoon down. "Done!"

"You're going to be hungry in the morning, you know." But she'd taken her bites. "You want her noodles, son?"

"*No-doos!*"

"All right." He poured out the broth and gave Noah the noodles. "Come on, girl. Let's get your butt in the bath." He'd plop Noah in the tub with Charlie as soon as he finished eating.

His phone rang before he even got around the pass-through, and he glanced at the screen, answering. "Hey, Angie! How goes it?"

"Hey, Sky. How would you like a baby for Christmas?"

"Pardon me?" Their baby was due the middle of January.

"Well, I know you have January down in your super organized little planner, but Junior seems to have decided to come a little sooner...ow. Oh, man. Yeah. Definitely sooner."

"Oh. Oh, wow. Okay. What do you need, honey?"

He flipped to his message app. *Home. You. Now. Baby coming. NOW BECK*

"Um. Maybe a ride to the hospital? Or...should I call 9-1-1? I don't know! Ow. It's your baby. What do you want me to do?" Angie sounded a little hysterical.

Dino isn't due until January

"Beck is on his way, lady. No worries."

You get your motherfucking ass to Angie's house RIGHT NOW or I will rip your balls off. I have 2 kids—1 is naked, 1 is covered in soup. GO NOW

Beck's reply came back instantly. *Yes sir OMW*

"Papa, bath time!" Charlie shouted from upstairs.

"Coming, Charlie! Bubba, come on. Bath. Beck is on the way, lady. He's got this. I'll come once I get a sitter for Thing One and Thing Two." Not panicking. *Call Lacey. Call Mom and Dad. Call Parker. Bathe children. Santa cartoons. Jesus fucking Christ.*

"Thank you, Sky. I'm fine. I'm breathing. I'm just...wow. I'm good. Thanks. Bye." Angie hung up, which was good because Noah was wiggling.

Then his phone rang, Lacey's name popping up.

"Hey, you. Did Beck call you?" He carried his wiggle monster upstairs and started the bathwater running while Charlie jumped up and down in the hallway. That got Noah jumping too.

"From the car. I'm packing a bag so I can stay the night. Or two. Whatever. Just relax, I'll be there soon." Lacey sounded cool as a cucumber. Not a hint of worry in her voice. "Merry Christmas, huh?"

"Lord have mercy. You know it. Just come on in. I'm bathing hooligans." He needed to gather the baby's little kit and put it in the car. Thank God he'd washed the dinosaur onesie-deal.

"See you soon." Lacey hung up.

"Jump!" Noah sang, falling on his butt every time he landed.

Charlie stuck her head into the bathroom. "I'm *cold*, Papa!"

"Water's run. Let's get in. No. Jumping." He put her in

first, then Noah, and sat on the pot as they splashed. Then he called Beck.

"Hold on. I'm putting you on the Bluetooth thingy." Beck promptly hung up on him instead.

"Oh, for fu—fire trucks." He called again. "Still me, Pappy!"

You hang up on me again, and I'm moving to China.

"Fuck. Sorry. Sorry about that, you know I hate this thing, I can never get it to—I'm almost at her house. I promise." The "Please don't rip my balls off" was implied.

"Good deal. Lacey's on her way. I'm fixin' to call your folks. I will meet you at the hospital with food and the car seat and all the stuff." He could so smoke a joint right now. *...No. No. Bad. Bad bad.*

"I'll call you when we get there and we know something. This is crazy. More crazy. I love you."

"I love you, babe. It'll be okay." He hoped. "I've got babies in the tub. See you soon."

They hung up, and he left Parker a message, then called the grands. *Babies babies babies.*

"Noah, don't kick your sister, it's not nice."

Noah giggled and kicked her again.

"Bubba, Papa said that's not nice." Charlie splashed him, and Noah splashed her right back.

"Sky? I'm here!" Lacey called from downstairs. "Where do you need me?"

"Up here! Hi, Dad. It's Sky. The baby is coming." He tagged Lacey into the bathroom and headed to put on a second layer and better socks.

"The baby can't be coming, it's not due until January. It must be false labor. Ali had that you know and—it's *Sky*. He says the baby is coming."

Here at Angs. Water just broke.

K. Coming

"Her water broke, Dad. The baby is coming."

Fuck fucking fuck fuckety fucker. Oh, that felt better.

"Did you say her water broke?" Mom was on the line now. "You better get to the hospital. Don't let us keep you. Call when you know something, please?"

"Will do. Lacey is here with the kids. Love y'all." He wasn't scared. Nope. Not even a little.

"Just breathe, kiddo. Mother Nature is in charge now. Love you too, Skyler. Bye-bye."

I wish you were here, I'm a fucking wreck. She doesn't know that. I'm good. Off to the ER. Love you.

Leaving now. Picking up burgers. CU soon

He headed back to the bathroom. "Okay, y'all. The dragon baby is coming, so I'm going to meet Pappy and meet her or him. Can y'all be good for Lacey? I told her y'all could watch cartoons."

"We'll be good Papa! Kiss the baby dragon!"

Noah blew him a kiss and waved. "Bye-bye!"

Lacey followed him out of the bathroom. "Don't worry about anything. I'm here as long as you need me. Unless we get to Christmas. Then we need to talk." She grinned. "Have fun. Good luck. Take pictures."

"I will." Oh. Phone chargers. They'd both need those.

He grabbed the cords and the plugs, along with both iPads on the way out the door. By the time he'd grabbed burgers, fries, Cokes and driven to the hospital, they were up in the maternity ward along with Keri, Angie's girlfriend, who'd brought pizza.

"I hate you all. Save me a slice and some fries for when this is over."

"Well. It's a party in here now." A tall woman in blue jeans and a Hello Kitty T-shirt came in. Her long, thick, dark hair was tied back, and she had cats-eye shaped glasses on.

"Hey, guys, this is Jane, she's the midwife on duty tonight."

"Oh, are these the dads?" Jane asked, not paying them all that much attention. She was busy checking monitors and putting on gloves. "Turn around, boys."

"Yup." Beck turned around so fast he was risking whiplash.

Sky chuckled and waggled his eyebrows at Angie before he turned, and she cracked up.

"At least I'm less hairy than a horse, right Sky?"

"I'm telling you, you are not the scariest female beast I've ever been near, lady." Nowhere near.

Jane was quick. "Okay, all clear. So. You're about four weeks early, which is not as scary as it sounds, but we're still going to watch you and baby pretty carefully. You're moving along fast so...we'll see what the doctor says. All the vitals are good. You should rest and let me know when you want pain relief. Any questions?"

"Can I have pizza?"

"No. Jell-O. Popsicles."

Angie sighed. "Orange?"

"I'll see what I can do." Jane smiled and waved as she headed out the door. "Be good, everyone. Back in a bit."

Sky turned and sat. "So, early bird. You couldn't wait until after Christmas?"

Angie rolled her eyes. "Maybe I want to be not the size of a house for Santa."

"Are you guys excited about your trip?" Beck asked, and Keri and Angie both nodded. They were planning to travel for a year or more—just see the world before they settled down.

"We were leaving in February, but now we could leave earlier and maybe see my folks first." Keri gave Angie a toothy grin.

"Oh, hell no." Angie laughed, then hissed. "Ooh. Fuck."

"Is there anything I can do to help, honey?"

"I took the classes with her. She just needs to remember to breathe, right?"

"Fuck off, Keri. You breathe."

Keri chuckled. "Just remember—Bondi Beach."

"I'm so fucking ready." Angie took a deep breath, eyes on Keri.

"Good, see? Breathing. Sand, sun, and a bevvie, eh?"

"Your accent sucks."

"Labor makes you so *grumpy*." Keri gave Angie a kiss. "I'm gonna see a lady about a popsicle. I'll be back."

"Are you guys excited?" Angie asked, her voice quavering. "I mean, you suddenly have two kids."

"And this is our dragon baby," Beckett said, with a wicked grin.

"Your what?"

Sky dug out the coming-home outfit. "Charlie picked it out. She says the baby is going to be our dragon."

"I can't promise any child genetically linked to me is going to be an angel..." Angie squinted and puffed out a breath. "But a dragon might be going a bit far..."

"Are you okay?" Beck moved to her side. "You look a little—"

"Where's Keri? Keri!"

"Hey!" He stood and took Angie's hand as Beck sprinted out the door. "Hey, lady. Look at me. You got this. You so got this. You're the strongest gal I know, and soon you'll be on the beach, sending me texts of the beautiful people while I'm up to my eyeballs in dirty diapers."

It was a little bit like chatter for a guy on the back of a bull, really. Just a calm distraction.

"Something's wrong."

A doctor in a white coat, Keri, Jane, and Beck came hurrying into the room.

"BP is up." That was followed by a bunch of quiet talk between the doctor and the midwife as Keri held Angie's hand.

And Beck had a death grip on his.

"Damn." Beck shifted from foot to foot nervously.

"Breathe, baby." He would not lose faith. This baby was meant to be. This was their dragon baby, and the good Lord would be with this doctor and make it work out.

The doctor put one hand on Angie's belly and one under the drape. Jane told her to take a deep breath and after a quick shove on one side of Angie's dragon bump, her BP went down quickly.

"Sometimes they get stuck. And that makes everybody cranky." The doctor stepped back. "You're getting close, you want that epidural?"

Angie nodded. Keri grinned and brandished an orange popsicle, and Angie snapped it up.

Sky took Beck's hand. "C'mon. No one wants us in here for this. We'll be in earshot, y'all need us."

Beckett needed a hug, and so did he. He was calm outside, but his heart was going, ninety to nothing.

"Okay, guys." Keri seemed relieved. "We'll make sure you don't miss the good part."

Beck gave the ladies a wave but didn't say anything, just followed him out of the room, and didn't seem to breathe until they were down the hall. "I am not cut out for that."

"We're guys." He pulled Beck into his arms, holding on tight. "I love you."

Beck hugged him hard. "I just love her so much already."

"Noah and Charlie are excited." He rested his forehead against Beck's. "I need her to be whole and healthy and home. I hear you, babe."

"I just...I sometimes feel like someone's punching bag since Connor died, you know? Like we can't have one single thing go easy. Not one damn thing."

He pondered that hard, then chose his words carefully, because he didn't want Beck to think he was just a hayseed with a Pollyanna complex. "I guess I can see that. You got more time on your own to worry right now than I do, but I think we're incredibly blessed. We got each other, we got our babies, we got enough money to spoil them, we got your people that love us, and we got another baby that wants to be here for Santa. Life's not supposed to be easy. It's supposed to be life, and ours is *amazing*."

Beck nodded and was quiet for a bit, also thinking hard. "I don't mean to sound ungrateful," he said softly. "And I'm not unhappy at all. We're lucky, you're right. And I don't know why I'm even looking for easy; you weren't easy to get, and you were even harder to get back. And the kids...the best things in my life have been well worth the work."

"It's just been a lot. A whole lot. Even good stress is stress, and losing Connor was a terrible shock." And God knew, Beck didn't get a chance to deal with it at all.

Beck sighed, then caught his eye and gave him a soft smile. "But we're having a dragon baby. And I'm not going to be sad today. I'm excited. A little terrified, a little anxious, but excited."

"Yep. Our dragon princess. Ours. And we'll take her home to a big brother and a big sister." He took a deep breath, but he couldn't stop grinning. "I want to hold her, but more than anything, I want to see the baby in your arms."

This time Beck's smile reminded him of the sun breaking over the Green Mountains—bright and fresh and young. "I can't wait. She's going to be beautiful." Beck winked. "Or he. He'll be just as gorgeous."

"Yes. Whoever will be perfect." Like the two that were waiting at home with Lacey.

"How about we get some coffee and check in on the kids?"

"Sounds perfect. I'll text Lacey—I bet they're out." They headed toward the nurses' station. "Did I tell you Noah ate a whole grilled cheese and all the noodles from Charlie's soup?"

"You're kidding." Beck shook his head. "That kid. Happy and hungry. Connor was six five, you know."

"Yeah, yeah." Sky was five four, in his boots. "Well, we better buy some cows to feed him."

Beck laughed. "He can juggle them to entertain us in our old age."

"Oh, I bet there's a place in the rodeo for a trick like that..." Cow juggling for fun and profit.

Beck eyed him playfully. "No. No rodeo children. You promised. Maybe the circus."

"Ooh, or Cirque. That would be grand. Free tickets." He chuckled at himself, at the thought of that little boy being grown, being a man.

Beck pulled out his phone and dialed Lacey. "Hey, how's it going?" Beck gave him a questioning look. "Charlie wants to sleep with you in our bed?"

"I don't care, honey." They had to get the guest room finished, in a hurry.

His phone beeped and it was Parker. *baby yet?*

Nope.

I'm about ten hours away. Have the trailer. Coming to help

He closed his eyes for a second. *Oh. Huh.*

"Go ahead. The sheets are in the skinny closet at the top of the stairs. Charlie loves to help make beds. And help yourself to anything, okay. Like usual. And don't be a stickler for the rules. Charlie's probably nervous. And—yes, sorry. I know. I am. Thank you. We'll keep in touch." Beck hung up the phone. "She told me to stop babbling..."

"Parker's coming with the trailer." He blurted the words out. Beckett and Parker had basically worked out their shit, mostly.

Beck blinked at him. "I'm sorry, I thought I just heard you say Parker was coming...with his trailer."

"He says he's on his way to help. I didn't ask him to come." He didn't. Hadn't. Hell, he'd just texted to say the baby was coming.

"We already have enough children." Beck sounded annoyed, but when Sky glanced over, his husband was grinning.

"I'll make him work for his supper." Parker could paint or play ball with Charlie or be Walter's scratching post.

"He can chop wood, wash dishes, clean up the basement..." Beck poured them each a tall cup of coffee to go, and a third one for Keri. "My parents aren't moving until January. I'm not going to argue with extra hands. I'll have to go back to the office a few times and wrap things up if I'm taking my leave early. It'll be good for you to have a friend around, so it's cool of him to want to help."

That was maybe the nicest thing Beck had ever said about Parker. They were friendly now, but Beck still loved to give him shit.

"I bet Charlie and Noah like him, too."

Beck laughed. "Of course they will. Everybody likes Parker."

Yeah. Parker worked very hard to make sure people liked him. Sky had to grin—well, Beckett sure hadn't liked the little shit. Not for a long time.

As if Sky would ever sleep with Parker. Parker was like a little brother. They could laugh now, but man, it hadn't been funny at the time. The way Parker told it, Beck had been ready to strangle him in Baltimore when Sky was in the hospital.

His man had been jealous. The idea was kind of hot.

Angie looked much more comfortable when they got to the room, way more in control.

"Better, lady?" Sky asked, and she nodded.

"Yeah. I love you two, but not that much."

Beck handed Keri her coffee, then took Angie's hand. "You are a rock star, you know that? I mean, I know it's a financial arrangement and blah, blah, blah...but this is hard. And we appreciate it. We're so excited."

"I'm glad. Seriously. I was worried that you'd back out after the accident, and I'm so glad you have room for three."

"Back out?" Beck looked shocked. "Never. That never once crossed our minds, I promise. That's a little baby Skyler in there. We'd make room for ten if we needed to."

They'd left the room to regroup at just the right time. His Beck was back, sure and confident.

Sometimes they all needed a hug, he guessed. It didn't hurt that Angie seemed much less frightened.

"Things are pretty chill now," Keri said. "She's all doped up, and we're watching the monitors. Her contractions are getting closer together." She glanced at the clock on the wall. "It's six o'clock now...so, are we taking bets? I'm going to say...ten-fifteen. Sky?"

"I'll go for one in the morning." One-two two-one was a fun birthdate, after all.

"Hm." Beck squinted, thinking. "I'll say two a.m."

"You guys. You're all so pessimistic. "I'll say...eight."

"Eight in the morning?" Keri asked.

Angie raised an eyebrow. "Eight tonight. Like, two hours from now."

"You're not going to have a baby in two hours, honey."

Angie crossed her arms and eyed Keri. "Watch me."

Beck laughed and gave them room, moving back to Sky's side. "I like twelve twenty-one."

"Me too. Our Christmas baby." He got a little goose-pimply. He was ready to see this little one.

14

"One more, Angie. That's it, just one more push."

Their little baby dinosaur was coming. Beckett was barely breathing and had both arms around Sky to keep himself grounded. This was the most amazing thing he'd ever seen. "Almost there, Stud."

"One more push." Sky took a deep inhale, and his husband's eyes were sparkling with tears. "Listen to that cry."

Keri hunkered down and pressed her forehead to Angie's temple. Angie took a deep breath and pushed.

"Yes! Good work. Relax, Angie. It's a beautiful girl. She looks great."

Beckett watched in awe and everything over the next few minutes seemed to happen in slow motion. The midwife took the baby—a girl just like Sky said it would be—and put her under a warmer, cleaned her a little, weighed her and recorded some numbers, then put the baby in Angie's arms.

"A very healthy baby girl," the midwife said, smiling.

Angie's eyes lit up. "Oh, she is pretty."

Beckett's fingers itched to hold her. He didn't know how

this was supposed to work, and it seemed mean to try to tear her from her birth mother's arms so soon no matter what their agreement said. He needn't have been so anxious, though, after a minute and a whispered couple of words with Keri, Angie looked at them. Her eyes were teary, but she was smiling.

"Come get her, Sky. She's yours."

"She is. Our Sierra Elizabeth." Sky smiled at Angie, meeting her eyes before he even touched the baby. "You did good, lady."

"Thank you. Take her, huh? I need time with my Keri."

Sky nodded and picked her up, bringing Sierra right to him. "Our little girl."

And then Sky gave her to him, easy as pie, and his baby was in his arms.

He couldn't help his gasp. He thought Sky would...he hadn't expected...

Oh, wow.

"Oh. Wow. Hi, Sierra. Hey, baby girl. Oh, look at you." She had crazy hair and her dark eyes blinked at him. He fought the tears, though he didn't know why. He was happy, and she was beautiful. He looked at Sky and didn't hide them anymore. "She is perfect."

"She is." Sky snapped a picture of them, then of the baby. "Lord have mercy."

Sky stroked her cheek with one finger.

He kept her cradled safely against him with one arm and pulled Sky in with the other. "Look what you made, Stud. This little girl is part...you."

"Us. She's ours. Our dragon baby." Sky took a deep breath and let it out. "What do we have to do to take her home, babe?"

"She has to stay tonight just to be sure she's okay, to get

her shots and to be seen by the pediatrician. Heath will have to come tomorrow afternoon to oversee all the paperwork and signatures, and as soon as the hospital will release her, we can take her home." He needed to call Heath, talk to his mom...but he wanted this moment just with Sky.

"We can stay with her, right? She needs to be with her dads. She's going to need to eat." Sky wasn't going to leave this hospital without their daughter, Beckett could tell.

"She's ours, Sky. She's ours right now. We can stay, we're her parents." He'd seen to that. The baby wasn't biologically Angie's—it was Sky's and a donor egg, so they had legal and physical custody the second Sierra had been born.

"Gentlemen, we need to take her for a few minutes to get her checked out and bathe her."

"We have to let her go?" Beckett frowned. He wasn't ready yet.

"Just for a little while. Do you want to come watch? You can stay just outside the nursery windows."

"We want to come." Sky held out one hand. "I'm Sky, and this is Beckett. We're the dads."

The nurse shook his hand. "I'm Clara, one of the night-shift nurses. It's good to meet you both. She's a beautiful baby, congratulations. Would you put her in her bassinet for me, please?"

Beckett nodded and set her down carefully. "We're right here, Sierra. Don't worry."

She fussed a little until Clara covered her and tucked a blanket tight over her middle. "Follow me, guys."

Skyler grabbed the bag of baby things and their chargers. "I didn't know if Angie would need her own space. I think I would." Then Sky took his hand and tugged. "Come on. I don't want her out of my sight."

"I do think Angie should have space. It's not our room,

it's hers, and I'm sure this is emotional for her. We'll have to manage." He let Sky lead him along and kept a tight hold of his cowboy's hand.

"Once she's cleaned up, you can feed her. We have a couple of unused rooms, I'm sure we can find a space for you to room-in with her overnight. Just give us a few minutes to figure it out."

Clara ducked through the doors into the nursery, rolling Sierra inside. "She won't be out of your sight, guys. No worries."

"We should video her bath. Mom will want to see." Sky forwarded his folks the pictures, eyes still on Sierra. "She's beautiful, isn't she? I can't wait for Charlie and Noah to meet her."

Sometime over Thanksgiving weekend, Sky had quietly transitioned from Laura and Tom to Mom and Dad, and it made Beckett smile.

"Mom will love every video you send her and ask for more." He stood behind Sky, letting Sky get the pictures while he took everything in. Remembering all of this seemed very important. "I hope they'll release her tomorrow, but if not I'll run home and get them so they can meet her."

His phone started blowing up, and he pulled it out of his pocket. "Speaking of, Mom got the pictures and sends thanks and love. Did you text Lacey to warn her that Parker and a trailer may show up tonight?"

"I did, yeah." Skyler was in love; Beckett could see it in the way he watched every motion the nurse made.

He leaned close to Sky's ear and slipped an arm around his husband's waist. "She is wonderful. She's brand new and ours, and we get to see her grow up from minute one. It's amazing, right?"

"It is. Is it weird that I wish Charlie and Noah were here to see her? I want them to love her too."

"No. You want our whole family together. I miss them too. Soon, baby." They watched Sierra's first bath, watched them dress her and get footprints.

"Look at her tiny feet!" Sky chuckled, obviously tickled. "Man, she's *pissed*."

Everything about her was tiny, and yeah, she wasn't happy, screaming her little tiny lungs out. "She's hungry, I bet."

"I hope they let me feed her. I want to hold her baby body."

"They will." And sure enough, Clara smiled and waggled a bottle at them before putting it in a warmer.

"Hey, guys, it's a quiet night. My supervisor said you can use one of the rooms. Just give me a second to get her bottle ready."

"Yes, ma'am. Thank you." Sky was damn near vibrating, voice husky as hell.

"How about that? We're so lucky."

Clara rolled the bassinet out just a few minutes later.

"This way." She handed Sky the bottle and headed down the hall in the opposite direction from Angie's room. "The drawers underneath her have diapers and wipes, a couple of clean onesies...all kinds of things you might need. I'll be back every two hours with another bottle."

She parked the bassinet in a small room. "The view isn't great, but it has a private bathroom." Clara looked at Sky. "Do you need me to show you how to feed her?"

"No, ma'am. I've been around little ones before." Sky shot her a wicked grin. "Cowboys make a lot of babies."

Clara snorted but grinned at him on her way out the

door. "Cowboys. Tell me about it. Have fun, guys. Call me if you need anything." She gave a little wave and left.

Beckett went right to Sierra. "It's just you and me and Sierra now. You want to sit, and I'll hand her to you so you can feed her?"

"I do. Please." Sky sat, looking at his hands. "What time was she born?"

"All her stats are on the tag here...uh...one twenty-eight a.m. You win." He grinned and carefully lifted their fussing, hungry baby into his arms. "Here she comes."

"Hey, baby girl." Sky brushed the nipple against her bottom lip. "Aren't you the sweetest baby girl? Are you empty as a worm?"

She stuck her tongue out and as soon as she tasted a little drop of milk, she sucked the nipple right into her mouth.

"Are there a lot of starving worms in Texas?" He joked, stroking a hand over Sierra's head.

"Tons. Millions." Sky chuckled. "She's a solid little critter, isn't she?"

"Almost seven pounds. Seems pretty solid to me. And it looks like she's a good eater. Noah will be pleased." He pulled up a chair beside Sky, just wanting to be close. "I guess I better go do some shopping tomorrow with that list we made, huh? Before we bring her home. Formula and diapers and those things."

"Yeah. And she needs a couple of blankets." One tear escaped Sky, dangling on his bottom lashes. "Sierra Elizabeth, dragon baby extraordinaire."

Beckett put an arm around Sky and kissed his temple. "I guess I better add dragon food to the list."

15

S ky had never been so scared as he was driving Sierra home.

Beckett was behind him in his car, and Sky fought the urge to hyperventilate. It was the longest drive of his life, and by the time he pulled into the driveway of their house, he was two seconds away from puking.

It didn't help that his old trailer was parked on the property. He wasn't ready for Parker.

To be honest, Sky wanted a nap.

The front door opened, and Charlie came out, running for all she was worth. "Papa! I missed you! Did you bring the dragon baby? Did you, Papa?"

"I did. Would you like to see her? She's wearing the outfit you picked out." He opened the car door and lifted Charlie up to see. "This is Sierra."

"She's sleeping," Charlie whispered.

He heard Beck get out of his Jeep. "Parker and I can get all the stuff, Stud. Why don't you go in and sit with her and the kids?"

"Can you hold the back door open for me, Charlie-girl? I

missed you and Noah so bad last night. I wanted my whole family together." He'd loved holding his newest daughter, but he'd wanted them all five home and safe.

"Yes, sir." Charlie's eyes were glued to her little sister, but she held the door like it was the most important job ever.

Lacey was there with Noah, who was fighting to get down. "Pappy! Want Pappy! *No! Pappy! Where you?*"

Sierra jerked and began to cry, and Charlie's eyes went wide. "Oh, baby. Oh, little baby sister. No."

"Hey there, buddy. I'm right here. Thanks, Lacey." Beck took Noah and that calmed their boy down a little. "How is my good boy? Is Parker in the trailer?"

Lacey nodded. "I invited him in for some coffee this morning, and he played with the kids for a while, but I think he needed a nap."

"Noah's mean. He woke her up." Charlie was watching Sky's every move.

"Noah's just excited. Let's sit on the sofa together and see if she won't go back to sleep." He sat and eased Sierra into his arms. "Come sit with me, Sister, and we'll rock her a little."

"Okay." Charlie climbed up next to him. "Can I touch her?"

"Yep. Just be super gentle because her skin is new." Sky figured that was a better word than delicate.

Charlie reached out carefully and patted Sierra's hair, then touched her cheek. "She's soft, Papa."

"Dragon!" Noah called out.

"Shh...quietly, Noah," Beck said gently. "Can you whisper? Then I can let you say hello to her."

Noah nodded. "Whisper." It wasn't quite a whisper, but it was quiet.

Beck sat on Sky's other side with Noah.

"Oh, I have to..." Lacey pulled out her phone and started taking pictures.

Charlie looked so serious. So very firm. "Noah. This is our baby. You can be a big brother. I am the most big sister."

Oh, that was adorable. The most big sister.

"Dragon," Noah said as if correcting her.

"That works too." Beck let Noah play with her feet for a second. "Okay, Noah. How about a bath before bed?"

"I can do that, Beckett. Charlotte, you were coming up for a bath too, remember?"

Charlie looked torn. "You take good care of her, Papa?"

"I promise to God, Charlie-girl."

She kissed Sierra's forehead and headed up with Lacey.

Beck looked over at him. "There are four adults in this house. We don't all have to be tired. I'll get the stuff out of the car, and then one of us should take a nap, right?"

"Uh-huh." Skyler stared at Beck. "We're home."

He couldn't believe it. He couldn't quite breathe.

"We're home." Beck slid a hand along his, where it was holding Sierra. "All of us."

There was a quick knock on the front door. "Hey, y'all," Parker called as he came in.

Beck chuckled. "All of us and Parker."

"Is this the newest member? Numbers one and two are amazing. Number three has a lot to live up to."

Sky snorted. "Hey, butthead."

"Congratulations." Parker knelt by the sofa and looked at Sierra. "Wow, you make pretty babies, man."

"I think so too," Beck said, offering Parker a hand to shake. "Good to see you."

"I can't stay but a couple days. I got to be in Raleigh Christmas Day, but I wanted to stop by, meet the kids, help for a day or two." Parker offered him a shit-eating grin. "Lacey is a sweetheart and a half, isn't she?"

Beck stared. "Did you change teams, Parker?"

"Nope. She's just nice. I mean, I can think someone's nice, right?" Parker rolled his eyes. "She offered me coffee and made me eggs."

"She is nice. She's more than nice, she's been a godsend. I don't know how we'd manage without her. She's been here for two days...she's upstairs putting the kids to bed for us right—" Beckett's phone chimed, and he hauled himself to his feet with a groan. "Feeding time. I'll get a bottle. Have a seat, Parker."

"Are you sure?"

Beck nodded and Parker sat to talk to Sky. "Hey, buddy. I hired a couple of carpenters and we have the basement painted, the guest room walls and door up. You need the trim up, and the furniture in, right? The laundry stays where it is, and there's a place where you can put a pool table or a gaming system and a sofa. Somewhere just for grown-ups."

Sky stared at Parker, not following. "What?"

"Merry Christmas, man. Happy new family. The guys took up a collection. I got a bunch of Christmas shit in the trailer too, for all y'all."

"Parker. You. I." Jesus, he was lucky. "Seriously?"

"Hey, it's not every day a good friend needs room for three kids in three months. Everybody wanted to do something, and this is what you needed." Parker shrugged, eyebrows waggling. "And I may have slept with the guy that does your day labor hires for the event a couple times."

"Oh, you horndog!" He started laughing, just tickled shitless.

"Friendly. I'm friendly." Parker touched his pinky finger to Sierra's hand, and she gripped it in her little fist. "She's so little. You must be pretty happy, huh? I gotta say, I really didn't expect the whole baby thing with you and Beckett, but it looks good on both of you."

"I didn't expect it, either, but I wanted it. I want to raise a family with Beck, and I'm doing it."

"Did you—I mean, do you feel different because she's yours?"

"No. She's special because she's Sierra, but Charlie is special because she's Charlie. And Bubba is special because he's Noah." He guessed he ought to think Sierra was the best, but Charlie and Noah were his now. They needed him too. They loved him, and he loved them.

"That's cool. They're lucky to have you guys. At least they're all real little so they can grow up together. They won't know any different. Maybe Charlie a little, but three or four years, I bet she doesn't think about it much at all."

"Think about what?" Beck came back in and handed him a warm bottle. "Is it too hot? I tried the wrist thing..."

"Whether or not Sierra's her dragon baby or not." He put the bottle to his cheek. "It don't feel hot to me."

"Well, we both know the answer to that. You want to feed her, Parker?"

"What?"

"Feed Sierra. With the bottle." Beck grinned.

Parker looked worried. "Me? She's kinda new for strangers, don't you think?"

Sky chuckled and shook his head. "It's weird. It's like I can't remember her not being here. I mean, yesterday she wasn't. Three months ago, Charlie and Noah weren't, but..."

He guessed that was how it worked. One day the world changed and normal changed with it.

"I can't even remember what I was doing at my desk before I got the call." Beck laughed.

"That's 'cause you ain't slept in two days, man." Parker held Sierra carefully and offered her the bottle. This obviously wasn't the first time Parker had done this; he had the technique down.

Beck nodded. "True. So true."

"Oh, she's a good eater. Look at her suck that in."

"She was born hungry. She was not waiting another few weeks, either. She wanted her first Christmas." Sky needed to make sure that Santa brought things for Sierra that the other kiddos could see.

"Only a couple of days away. And it sure is cold enough. Santa will be glad for a warm chimney. Right, princess?" Parker waggled the bottle and grinned at Sierra. "Yes, Santa will come for you too. Never too late to be added to the list."

"Nope. We'll have to get her a Christmas dress to match Charlie's so I can get pictures." Beck's folks were not happy to be missing this Christmas, but they had other grandbabies to be with.

"We'll get Noah a little sweater to match." Beck laughed. "Oh, God. We're those parents."

"Of course you are, Beck," Parker said, laughing. "Look at you. Even after a sleepless night at the hospital, both your socks match."

Beck snorted. "Funny. Just because I actually own two matching socks..."

"All my socks match." All his socks were basically white, for the most part.

Parker looked appalled. "Oh, you've ruined Sky now too."

"We bring out the best and the worst in each other." Beck sat next to Sky, squeezing in between him and the armrest, and tucked an arm around his back. "Hey, you. Are you hungry?"

"Who, me?" He didn't think so. He wasn't sure. He knew he didn't want to get up.

"Yes, Stud. You. The only man I'll brave the kitchen for." Beck kissed his cheek. "I'll bring you a sandwich. You can decide after you take a bite. And then you can have the first nap. We can take shifts. Deal?"

"I guess, yeah." To be honest, he was so tired he wasn't tired anymore.

"I can stay until Christmas Eve morning but then I have family stuff..." Lacey appeared, looking rested and smiling.

"You're a rock star, Lacey. Thank you."

"No problem. Seriously. I'm looking forward to helping out." Lacey grinned at them both. "Right now, though, Charlie needs her papa, and if Pappy doesn't go read to Noah, he's going to have a breakdown."

"Oh, boy. No breakdowns allowed. Thank you. Parker, do you mind looking after Sierra for a little bit? Lacey could probably use a break."

"We're okay. Seriously. Lacey can spell me if it gets crazy."

Sky headed up to see his Charlie-girl. "Hey, angel girl. I missed you so bad."

She held her arms open, and he scooped her up. "Papa. Papa. Papa."

"Charlie. Charlie. Charlie." He held her, sitting on her bed and rocking her gently. "Mmm...I love you."

"I love you. You're home now, right? And Santa can come."

"In three sleeps, Santa will come. Three."

"Lacey helped me make a list for Santa for baby sister." Charlie looked at him. "Because I made one for Noah so it's fair now. She wants a squishy doll, a pacifier, and a pink spoon. Like Noah's spoon but pink. And I want to give her a dragon like mine that Grampa bought me."

"Oh, that's a great idea. What do you want to give Noah?" They snuggled down together on her bed.

Charlie looked at him, dead serious, and said, "A piano."

"A piano?" Okay. They had little kid keyboards at Target. He'd send Parker. "Does he like music?"

Charlie nodded. "Yes. And he likes to sing. He sings a lot." She yawned and tucked her fingers into his shirt. "A *lot*."

"Yeah, I hear you." He cradled her, covering her up. "We need to draw a picture for Pappy, too, to put on his desk."

He blinked nice and slow. She was warm, heavy, and sleepy.

"Maybe of the family. Maybe Lacey too. She's like family." She sighed. "Can I make eggs tomorrow?"

"Mmm...I'd love that. Your eggs are the best." He patted her back nice and easy, and she matched the touch on his chest.

Charlie went quiet, and a few minutes later he recognized the slow, even breathing that he knew meant she'd fallen asleep. The room was dim and silent, and it was hard not to fall asleep right there with her.

He saw Noah's light go off, and he told himself to get up. He should totally get up.

This was him. Getting up.

Beckett came into the room quietly and leaned over to kiss Charlie's forehead. Then Beck kissed him too. "You look so comfortable. Go to sleep. We'll trade off in a few hours."

"You sure? She wants to get Noah a piano and Sierra a baby dragon for Christmas." He yawned until his jaw popped. "We're all home. All of us. Thank God."

"I'm grateful. I'm relieved too. And I don't think I've ever loved you more." Beck gave him another kiss, a slow one to say good night.

"I'll be down in a few. I just need a few minutes."

Just a couple.

He closed his eyes, snuggled in with his Charlie, and crashed like a lead balloon.

16

"There are four trucks in the driveway." Beckett shuffled into the kitchen in search of coffee after a five-hour nap. He'd call it a night's sleep, but it was more like a mini-coma than sleeping. He'd crashed; then he'd hauled himself out of bed.

"There are half a dozen guys in your basement too." Lacey grinned, bringing him a mug of coffee. "I heard you coming down the stairs."

"You're an angel. Where's—"

Lacey pointed to the couch where Sky was feeding the little dinosaur. "God, they're cute."

"He handles her like he was born to be a father, right?"

Beck nodded. "I think he was. I think maybe most cowboys are."

Charlie and Noah were sitting right up close, talking to Sky, at least until Noah saw him. "Pappy!"

Then he had to hand his coffee off because a little boy launched toward him.

"I got you!" He caught Noah mid-leap, impressed that he had any reflexes at all this morning. It was morning still, right? He hugged Noah, poking him in the tummy. "How do you like Sierra?"

"Baby dragon dragon baby sister!" Noah smiled, looking pleased with himself.

"That's her." This kid. "Morning, Charlie. Are you helping?"

"Uh-huh. I showed her my dragon from Grampa. She pooted." Charlie giggled hysterically.

He chuckled. "She does that. She gets it from Papa."

"That's what Uncle Park said!" Her eyes went wide. "Did you see downstairs? It's so neat!"

"Not yet. I knew he had some guys coming to work but... I guess I should go check it out. Have you been down there yet, Stud?" He gravitated toward Sky, wanting to be close. He didn't mind tired as much with Sky next to him.

"Yeah. I went down early. Lord knows how it looks now. Parker's making a run to the Target and the Lowes real quick."

"Wow. That's amazing. I can't believe he pulled this together so fast." Now that Noah was settled on his hip, he went back for his coffee before sitting with his husband. "I feel a little like we just ran this crazy sprint, and now we're warming up for a marathon."

"Tell me about it." Sky eased Sierra up onto a rag. "Okay, Sister. Let's burp her. Nice and easy."

"Yes. Pat pat pat, get out the bubbles."

Noah leaned over to pat too. "Easy, buddy. That's it."

And there was Lacey again, like their own personal photographer, snapping pictures on her phone.

Beck looked at her. "Lacey, you must be exhausted." She didn't look it, though.

"No. I'm good. I just sleep when those two sleep, and I'm golden."

"Oh. Cool." Noah made a dive for the baby with both hands and Beck caught him and stood, barely saving his coffee. "Easy buddy. She's fragile." He set Noah down in baby jail so the kid could run and went in search of some breakfast. "What time is it?"

"Ten till noon. The perfect time." Sky winked at him.

"Almost naptime," Lacey nodded, sagely.

"I guess I'm looking for lunch, then. You let me sleep too long." He didn't think too hard, just dug out stuff for sandwiches for everybody. He wasn't about to get creative today. Maybe takeout for dinner. Chinese or sushi. "I'm making turkey sandwiches for everyone, Charlie. Are you in?"

"Just cheese, Pappy? Please?"

Noah followed her. "Cheese! Cheese!"

"I think I can do that." He was working on getting her to eat sandwiches instead of roll-ups. They were easier to grab on the run. He'd made cheese for Noah too, but Noah would eat whatever got put on his tray. The kid just liked food.

"You want me to put her down, Sky?" Lacey's calm, capable presence was like a miracle right now.

"Yeah. I need to have lunch with my big kids. Thank you, lady. I appreciate it."

"Are you going to have turkey, Papa?" Beck teased. "Or just cheese?"

"I want it all."

"Greedy." Beck watched Sky carefully. Stress and anxiety weighed on his husband physically—not that Sky would ever admit that—so Beck was keeping an eye out. Being tired wasn't so great for Sky's hip either.

But happy was good for everyone, and they had plenty of that right now.

"Papa, we have to make Christmas cookies today. And

you have to make sure there's milks." Charlotte was very worried about her position with Santa.

"We have milk. Are you up for making cookies, Papa? Maybe we could ask Lacey..." He remembered Sky said he wanted to go shopping. "Lacey and I could do cookies, I bet."

"I was thinking that we could get the ones you slice and bake. Easy-peasy and they're pretty. We can decorate them with colored sugar?"

"Ooh...can I do it?" Charlie's eyes lit up.

"I don't see why not."

"Perfect." He didn't even know there was such a thing. "This is why I keep you around. So resourceful. That and you make pretty babies." *Babies? Baby?* He pushed that thought away, not a great time to be thinking about that.

Sky chuckled and kissed the top of Noah's head, pushing the mangled mass of cheese and bread back into play. "I'm going to make a list and get a delivery. Parker did all the special shopping earlier. This is just food."

Oh. Fantastic. Parker was a solid friend to Sky, and it was great that Sky was getting support from his crew. "Parker is handy, huh? I'm glad he came. Like, actually glad." He winked at Sky, slid him a sandwich, and then made one for himself.

"Thanks, babe." Sky fell on the sandwich like he was starving.

His man's appetite was healthy. That was a good sign. "I was thinking about asking Lacey to stay late so we could get a little hot tub in before bed. What do you think?"

"Oh, my hip might could handle that..." That was pure lust in Sky's expression.

He let himself stare right back, making sure Sky knew he

was on that train. It felt amazing to know Sky needed him. He was craving his cowboy. "I'll ask her after the kids go down for their naps." He changed the subject because his voice was getting husky. "How was that sandwich? Did you even chew?"

"Chew? What is this chew you speak of?"

"You want another one? Or here, maybe some chips? I was going to have a couple." He pulled a bag out of the cabinet and set it in front of Sky.

Noah made grabby hands, and Sky chuckled.

"We say please, Bubba."

Noah banged his high-chair tray. "Peas, Bubba!"

He chuckled. "Sounds about right."

"Bubba. No banging. That's not polite." Charlie modeled her very best manners. "Can I please have some chips, Papa?"

He heard his mother in his head saying, "We say may I, Beckett," but he kept his mouth shut.

"You surely can." Sky passed out a few chips to both kids.

"She went down easy. She'll be up again in a couple of hours I know, but for now, dads get a break." Lacey reached over and snagged a slice of cheese.

"I made you one." Beck tapped a plate at the end of the counter.

"Ooh. Thank you."

"So, Lacey." Beck leaned on the counter and smiled at her.

Lacey winced jokingly. "Uh-oh."

"Ha. Since tomorrow is your last morning with us for a while, I wondered how you might feel about staying the night so Sky and I could, you know, rehab his hip in the hot tub and get a little bit of sleep."

Lacey laughed. "Rehab is a very important adult activity."

Okay, she got it. Cool.

"I'm happy to be here, and then we're good until the second, right?"

"Yes, and my parents will be arriving sometime around the first. They move into their condo that first week of January."

"So soon?" she asked, and Sky nodded to her.

"That house of theirs sold quick."

"I think they took the first offer. They're anxious to be here." Technically his paternity leave was set to start that first week of January, but he would need to spend some time at the office after the holidays to finish what he'd left on his desk when he'd run out.

But he'd be home between Christmas and New Year's because it was just him and Sky, and they were going to be very outnumbered.

"Granny and Grampa want to meet the dragon baby and see me and Bubba." Charlie sounded completely satisfied with herself.

"You're right, they do. You're very important to them, and they miss you." He wasn't sure why or how these kids took to his family so well, but he was glad. Charlie was holding on tight, and he wanted to make sure she knew she was completely theirs now. Mom and Dad had sent presents, which were hidden along with all the things they'd tagged from Santa.

"Hey, y'all." Parker appeared from the basement. "You want to come tell us where to put the furniture?"

He looked at Sky. "There's furniture?"

Sky's grin was pure wicked joy. "Merry Christmas, Beckett."

"What?" He looked at Lacey. "Can you—"

"Go!" She grinned like she'd been in on the secret.

He took Sky's hand. "Show me."

Sky led him downstairs to a totally transformed space. The laundry had its own room with tables for folding and a sink; there was a gorgeous guest suite with a bathroom, and a little man cave with a double recliner, a little TV, and a video-game system. "There's a queen bedroom set, a rocker, plus a hide-a-bed for extra folks. Just tell them where to put it all."

"Sky...Parker, this is amazing." They'd cleaned up down here and marked out where they wanted things, but Parker and his crew had practically performed a miracle as far as he was concerned. He walked into the guest room and looked around, then ducked into the bathroom. "Oh, man. This is crazy. Okay...so the bed on that wall, dresser here. Rocker in that corner? You think?"

"I think that'll be perfect. It's a great space for people to stay, plus a little space for us if we need it." Sky leaned against the doorframe. "I wanted to have it all done before Sierra got here."

"Turn your backs if you embarrass easily, gents, I'm going to kiss the hell out of my husband." He was joking; he didn't care who saw. He grinned and tucked an arm around Sky's waist, pulling him close. "Pucker up, Stud."

"Merry Christmas, babe." Sky kissed him, easy as you please, no hesitation.

He felt like his heart was going to explode. Emotion leaked out his eyes, the salty tears mixing with their kiss. He couldn't help it—sure, he was tired, but it was more that he didn't have words to express everything he was feeling anymore. It was all too big. "I love you."

"I love you."

"Okay, dry it up. I got to get this done. I'll put all the new Santa stuff in y'all's man cave. I found another dragon doll, as requested."

Sky went to Parker and hugged him tight. "I owe you, man."

"Let me come visit after the first of the year."

"Always."

Beck rolled his eyes and wiped them on his sleeve. "You can come and stay any time, Parker. Thank you so much." He followed Sky's hug with one of his own, gratified that Parker actually hugged him back.

"You make him so fucking happy, man. It's so good."

"It is good. It's all good, all of it. We'll get out of your way. Thanks again, this is incredible. I'm just...stunned. I can't wait to use the man cave." The double recliner was awesome.

They could bring the baby monitor down and just be in the quiet.

He followed Sky upstairs, leaving Parker and his team to finish up. By the time they got upstairs, Lacey had the kids settled in for naps and had stretched out on the couch in the office to catch a nap herself.

Smart girl.

"It really does take a village, huh?" A village from all over.

"It does. I-I don't know how to thank you, babe. I didn't believe I could have this. I didn't know it was possible." Sky looked so raw, so open.

"I'd thought about it. A kid or two...but I certainly never imagined all of this." He drew Sky close again. "What a journey we're on now."

"Together. That's all I need. You and me and our family, together."

"Our first Christmas is going to be something else." Santa and two-hour feedings and dinner and...maybe even snow. It was going to be chaos. Fun, but crazy.

"All our Christmases will be. Thank God."

Beck pulled Sky over to the couch and sat them down, making sure Sky looked him in the eye. "You are an amazing father, you know that, right? It's good to be grateful, but you shouldn't be shocked. You deserve this. These kids are lucky to have you."

"I'm just trying to be—a good dad. I want them to know they're loved." There was a wealth of pain in those words, but there wasn't anything Beck could do but love Sky and have the man's back.

"I know." He caught Sky's cheek with one hand. "And you are. You know how I know? Charlie wants you to tuck her in every night. Noah giggles every time you smile at him. And Sierra? She doesn't eat as well for me. Our kids love you. You can relax. You've got this." Sky didn't need to make it hard, he just needed to be himself. That was all the kids wanted.

"I like it. I mean, I really like being a daddy. I didn't know if I would, but..." Sky shrugged and kissed him. "I do."

"Me too." Beck smiled. "That's a good thing, because we can't return them to Walmart."

"We can't? Dammit!" God, he loved that smile. He'd work for that smile. He'd do anything to make sure it stuck around. Anything Sky needed.

"You know, we have maybe forty-five minutes until the dragon wakes up." Beck put his feet up on the coffee table and leaned back in the cushions, pulling Sky with him. "We could snuggle for a few."

"Mmhmm...I like that plan. I love the way you smell,

Beck. It settles my soul." Sky cuddled in, the sigh soft and happy.

Right now, he probably smelled like a new father who hadn't showered in three days, but he'd take it. He liked knowing he was what Sky needed. He'd always liked Sky's compliments too; they made him feel tall and broad-shouldered. "I love the way you fit into my arms. There's a Sky-shaped spot just for you."

Sky kissed his chin, body going heavy against him, and Beck closed his eyes, soaking in the warmth and weight of his husband.

17

"I'm glad we decided to forego the wine; I think I might have fallen asleep." Beck followed Sky into their bedroom, talking quietly so he didn't wake anyone up. They had been on their feet and going all day and Sky had been pretty sore, but he was hoping their soak in the hot tub had helped his husband some. "It was nice to relax, though. Feeling any better?"

"I'm solid as a rock." Sky rolled his shoulders, slipping the robe off and exposing the sweet perfect body, that tight ass. Even with the scars, the surgeries, Sky was perfect to him.

"I'm glad. It's been a long couple of days." Long days, but he was looking to make this one just a little longer. He closed the door, and, ever hopeful, he locked it. He reached for Sky and traced the jagged angle of a scar on one shoulder, one of many he knew by heart.

"All healed." Sky stretched for him, leaning back against Beck, so nice and warm.

"I know." That one healed years ago. Right after they were married. "Still just as sexy." He kissed Sky's shoulder above the scar and slid out of his robe, letting it drop to the floor. "Just as tasty too." Beck licked that same spot and rested his hands on Sky's narrow hips.

"I like when you taste, baby. I like it a lot." There was the husky, wanton tone he loved to hear in Sky's voice.

"Yeah." His hands roamed over Sky's abs and chest, and he let his husband feel a little of his need, rocking into Sky's ass. "I know what you like."

"Mmm...you do. I want you, hmm, but you know that." Skyler slowly climbed up onto the bed, offering that pretty ass to him.

"Damn, Stud. I am never going to get tired of that view." Sky had his number. He would give his man anything he wanted. He moved up next to Sky and stretched out, looking for a kiss, craving their connection.

Sky settled beside him with a soft sigh, easing the hip, and he reached down, loving on his cowboy. There was nothing like Sky's kisses. Nothing like the slow exploration of his lips.

He knew they wouldn't get a lot of uninterrupted hours for a while so he focused on Sky, telling himself that no matter what came their way, this wouldn't change. He took his time and touched all the little places that made Sky shiver—the soft spot under Sky's jaw, the little hollow in his collarbone, the sensitive skin under one nipple. "It's good to have some time, isn't it? I've been missing you a little. This. You know what I mean."

"I do. Missing being adults. Together. Naked. Hard." Yeah, Sky understood completely.

"That. All of that." Beckett pushed his fingers into the curls at the base of Sky's cock and teased. "The hard bit especially."

Sky cupped Beck's balls, rolling them firmly enough that he felt it in the soles of his feet. "Tell me about it."

"Mmm. God that feels good." Beck curled his fingers around Sky and got a firm grip. Sky's cock was hot and hard, and he loved knowing he could do that.

"Yeah. Yeah, baby." Sky scooted closer, bringing them so close they could rub together, drag their skin together. Then Sky grabbed his cock and started jacking him in time.

"Fuck." He groaned and arched into Sky's hand. Sky smelled good, felt good, it had been a while since he'd felt all that skin.

"Mmm...love how your cock feels in my hand." Sky licked his lips and moaned as the kiss deepened.

"Me too." He was having trouble focusing. "I mean, yours too. I mean...fuck. Sky."

"Anytime. Fuck Sky. Suck Sky. Touch Sky."

He needed to work harder if Sky was that coherent.

He kissed his way to Sky's shoulder and found that tasty spot again, the one he'd wanted to get his teeth into earlier, and this time he didn't hold back. "Mm. Shout, Sky?" He bit around the muscle there, doing his best to suck up a mark Sky could admire in the morning.

Sky bucked, his hand clenching around Beck's prick. That was a sight, Beck's cowboy lost in pure sensation.

He grunted, eyes crossing as he worked his cock in Sky's tight grip. He let go and bathed the hot spot with a hungry tongue, making sure Sky got plenty of friction.

"Love you. Here." Sky scooted and suddenly both their cocks were in that strong, grasping hand.

Fuck, yeah. "Love you." He didn't try to hide the need in his voice. He braced a hand on Sky's hip and took another kiss, pushing his tongue past Sky's lips. Sky let him in, working their pricks, making a perfect circle between them.

Their grunts and pants were all he heard as his need built and his focus narrowed. *Close*, he thought, but he was too lost in their heavy kiss to say it.

Sky's thumb dragged over his slit, pushing just hard enough for a zing.

"Fuck!" He wanted to shout but it was more of a harsh whisper. His whole world was need and heat and Sky. Sky was all of it. He bucked into Sky's hand, fingers digging into Sky's hip as he shot.

An answering heat splashed against him, and the scent of Sky's spunk was just perfect—rich and male, right.

"Fuck. So perfect." He pressed kisses into Sky's throat between shallow breaths. "So good."

"Uh...uh-huh. Good." Sky was already baby-headed, blinking slower and slower.

He reached down and pulled a blanket up, covering them both. They could clean up later, but it was going to cool off fast in their bedroom. God, he was tired, and the blanket felt like it weighed a thousand pounds. "Love you. You're everything I need, Stud."

"Need you, baby. Can't do it without you." Sky blinked once more; then his eyes closed.

"Won't have to." He settled, sighing. "Not ever."

18

"Papa. Papa, Santa Claus comes tonight!"

Skyler looked up from where he was changing Sierra and encouraging Noah to sit on his potty. "He does. I think we'll watch cartoons today. All our Christmas ones."

"Where's Pappy?"

"He's grabbing some groceries. There's a big snowstorm coming, and we're going to enjoy it together." And they needed milk, diapers, and something easy for breakfast tomorrow.

"Oh. Where's Lacey?"

"Home with her family." He waited for the next question, sliding Sierra back into her onesie.

"Where's Daddy?"

"In Heaven with Jesus."

"Uh-huh." Charlie's grin was huge. "And where's Granny?"

"In California with your auntie." He scooped Sierra up. "Did you poop yet, Bubba?"

"No!"

"Okay. We'll wait." He sat in the rocker.

"Papa! Where's Grampa?"

Wishing he had snow and beer for Christmas. "With your granny."

"Uh-huh. And where's Uncle Park?"

"Driving to North Carolina." He loved this game.

Charlie climbed up next to Sierra. "Where's Papa?"

"Here with his Charlie and his Noah and his Sierra, where he belongs."

"Noah potty!" Noah waved like they'd forgotten he was there.

"He's *never* going to go." Charlie flopped in his lap. "Ugh."

"He might not, but it's good to practice, right?" That's what he'd read. Noah liked the potty chair—or he liked being naked, six of one or half dozen of the other...

"I guess," she conceded and rolled her eyes. "I think he likes to play with his winky."

He did not laugh. He didn't. He also didn't say, "All boys do."

He did say, "Lord have mercy," because what else could he say?

"Poop!" Noah stood up and looked into the little potty. "Little poop!"

"Ew. Stinky!" Charlie held her nose.

"Good for you, Bubba! Good deal!" He put Sierra in her crib for a second. "Let's wipe your butt and flush this. Good job!"

Beck would be tickled as all get out. Or horrified. You could never tell.

"Wipe my butt!" Noah wiggled his naked tush at Sky. "Bye-bye poop!"

Charlie groaned. "Noah. We don't talk about poop; it's gross!"

Sky got him into the bathroom, wiped him up, and waved to the poop as they flushed. Then he sent Noah for Pull-Ups and cleaned up the potty chair. Lord have mercy.

Scoop up baby, drag kids downstairs, and get one bottle, two sippy cups, two snacks, and a beer.

Oh, he should wait on the beer...

Sierra started fussing in her crib, and Charlie poked her head into the bathroom. "Dragon sister is hungry."

"How about you, girl? You ready for a snack? Bubba?"

"Gofish!" Noah waved a Pull-Up at him. "Milk."

"Can I please have," Charlie said with great emphasis and looking right at her brother. Then she looked back at Sky. "An apple and peanut butter?"

"You totally can. That actually sounds really good. I may have the same thing." Somehow, miraculously, he got all three children dressed and downstairs.

God, when was Beck coming home?

By the time Beck's Jeep pulled into the driveway, snack time was over, Noah was playing with blocks in baby jail, Charlotte was watching Christmas cartoons, and he had just finished giving Sierra her bottle.

"What a zoo! And it's snowing now, did you see?" Beck came inside, followed by a rush of frigid air. Beck set everything down on the kitchen floor and looked at him. "Whoa. You okay? Was it crazy? Sorry, the store was crowded."

Bruiser padded over and nosed at the bags, and they both bent reflexively and scooped them up, setting them on the counter instead.

"Noah pooped in the potty, Pappy, and the baby had a bottle, and me and Papa had apples and peanut butter."

Sky thought Charlie summed it up pretty well, really.

"I poop! Bye-bye poop!"

Beck leaned in and took a quick kiss. "Poop, huh?" Beck waggled his eyebrows, then hurried over to Noah, scooped him up, and danced him in a little circle. "Bye-bye poop? Great job, buddy!"

Noah squealed and giggled, arms going around Beck's neck.

"Boys." Charlie rolled her eyes and settled deeper into the sofa.

Three going on thirty. They were in so much trouble.

Beck hung on to Noah and gave each of the girls a smooch too. "I got everything on the list, plus candy canes for the tree and mini-marshmallows for our cocoa."

"Oh, you rock. I love cocoa."

Charlie's eyes lit up. "Me too, Papa."

"Me! Me Papa!"

He nodded to Noah. "You too, Bubba."

"Charlie, did you see it's snowing?" Beck pointed out the glass doors in the family room. It had been a slow start to the ski season, but it was really coming down now. "Are you going to build a snowman with me tomorrow?"

Beck looked like he instantly regretted asking when Charlie started singing. "Put on *Frozen*! Please?"

Noah bounced in Beck's arms. "Peas!"

"Oh, boy. We haven't seen that in at least...what, Papa? A day or two?"

Good thing he liked cartoons—the next decade of his life was going to be about poop, animation, and learning to fix hair. "It's been at least an hour and a half. How about Olaf's Christmas...thing? It's on here."

"Warm hugs." Noah reached for Sky, nearly launching himself out of Beck's arms.

"Whoops. Trade you." Beck took Sierra off his hands. "That was a close one. Hello, sweet thing. How is my baby girl?" Sierra's mouth went square like she was going to cry but Beck started bouncing and walking. "No, no we're not going to cry. Nope. Not my baby girl."

"She's going to cry," Charlie muttered, and Sky leaned to whisper into Noah's ear.

"Let's get her, Bubba."

Then they pounced on Charlie, tickling her and making her laugh hard.

"Stop! Bubba!" Charlie twisted and wiggled. "Papa!" She tried to tickle him too, but she couldn't reach. "I'll get you!"

He hugged her tight, then leaned back, arms spread. "Do your worst, kiddos!"

She attacked him, little fingers scrabbling against his ribs. Noah was trying too, tickling under his chin with a light touch, and giggling madly.

He let himself laugh and twist, pretending to be ticklish, which tickled the living shit out of the little ones.

Beck was laughing softly from a few feet away, but the baby was quiet, which was a good sign. He probably didn't want to wake her up.

Charlie sat back, grinning at him, cheeks pink. "We got you."

"Can you breathe, Papa?" Beck teased.

"I can, just barely." He winked over at his husband. "They are amazing ticklers, did you know?"

"I didn't. I am going to have to beware." Beck pointed to the kangaroo pouch Lacey gave them as a baby gift. He'd pulled it on and snugged Sierra right down in it, and she was sound asleep. "How about this?"

"I tried to figure that, but I couldn't get it for love or money. Go you!" He'd have to get Beck to help him figure it. Later.

Beck picked up the remote and turned on the TV, then

helped Sky sit up. "I know you said you wanted to put on a movie, but..." He searched and found *How the Grinch Stole Christmas!*

"Me and Papa read that one!" Charlie cheered, shocking Sierra awake.

"Shh. Hey baby. You're good. I got you." Beck rubbed Sierra's back, but she was mad now. "I'm gonna...where is her NUK? Is there one down here?"

"Charlie-girl, grab your sister's plug for me please?"

"Yes, sir!" She hopped up and grabbed it.

"Thanks, Sister." Beck teased Sierra's gums with it until she was interested, and she sucked it right in. Just a few more little whimpers and her eyes closed again. "There we go. Now, no shouting okay, girlie?"

"Sorry. You aren't going to tell Santa on me, are you?"

"Oh, hey." Beck took her hand and pulled her closer, talking quietly. "You're not in trouble, sweetie. We're all learning how this baby thing works. You and your brother are my first children, but Sierra is my first baby. I have a lot to learn too. We're all going to make mistakes."

Beck was talking to Charlie, sure, but he sounded a little like he might be trying to convince himself too.

"Everybody makes mistakes, y'all. Aren't any of us perfect." Sky fluttered his eyelashes like a giant butthead. "Except me, of course."

"Perfectly weird, maybe." Beck snorted and looked at Charlie. "Santa's going to come, and you and your brother and sister are going to wake up to snow and presents. Don't you worry. I promise."

Charlie looked at Beck, then turned to him. "You promise too." It wasn't a question. It was a demand from a worried little girl.

"I swear to God. Santa is coming tomorrow."

She beamed and leapt into his arms. "I love you. I love Pappy. I love Christmas!"

Beck reached over and touched a finger to her lips and winked dramatically. "Me too. But remember, Dragon Baby is sleeping."

Bruiser sighed from where he was lying in the middle of the room, patiently letting Noah climb all over him. "Oh, don't you complain, boy. We know better." Bruiser loved the kids.

"Good good boy, Bruise." Noah patted the pup, so gentle.

"And Walter. He's good." Charlie chimed in. "Good boy, Walter."

Walter opened one eye from his perch up high on the cat tree and closed it again.

"He's the best boy. Right, Walter?" Beck's complement got a flip of the tail. "Okay. Grinch. Ready?"

Noah clapped his hands, plopped down on his butt, and leaned against Bruiser.

Sky kissed the top of Charlie's head. "Love you, girlie."

"I love you, Papa."

Beck leaned toward him. "What's on the agenda? Do we need to cook? Did you need me to clean up anything upstairs?"

"Upstairs is glorious. I was thinking about ordering pizza. It's always been our tradition, huh?" Sky loved those weird little things like that.

"I love our Christmas Eve pizza. Maybe we can sneak in a beer." It was often more than one but...maybe not this year.

"Sounds perfect. One cheese and one deluxe?" He frowned, suddenly remembering the food. "Did you need help putting up the groceries, or did I just miss it?"

"Oh, sh—ugar. They're still on the kitchen counter." Beck peered at Sierra, then at Charlie. "Oops."

"I'll grab it. I need a coffee anyway. How about you?" He stood up and stretched, his back popping, his hips growling.

"Sounds great. Maybe a snack?"

Charlie shifted right over to Beck without complaint as he got up. Not to be left out, Noah climbed up on the couch too, and Beck was suddenly buried in children. All four of them had their eyes on the TV. It was pretty adorable.

Sky took a picture and sent it to Mom on his way to the kitchen. He put the food away, ordered the pizza, and made a quick plate of nachos for them all to nibble on.

"That smells good." Beck sniffed as he came into the room.

"Mmm. Cheese." Charlie was spot on with that remark as she reached for the chips.

"Cheese is a wonderful thing, especially once gooified." Sky snuggled right in, happy as all get out.

"Did I hear you ordering dinner?" Beck reached for a chip. "I was thinking we—"

The room went quiet as the TV shut off.

Beck felt around on the couch. "Did somebody sit on the remote?"

Charlie frowned. "Where'd Grinch go?"

"Oh. Damn. Sky, I think...is the electricity out? The cable box is dead."

"I'll go check the breaker box." At least they had gas and could drive the kids around in circles with the cartoons on if they had to.

"Hopefully that's all it is." Beck climbed out from under Charlie and put Noah in his pen as Sky headed for the basement. "But we have a few hours until dark and the wood stove will warm us up in here, at least."

"That's right. We're more than capable of sitting and snuggling and listening to carols on the phone." He jogged down the stairs and looked. Nope, all good there. *Dammit.*

"What's up, Stud? Did anything trip?" Beck called to him.

"No, babe. Check for outages?" He headed back up the stairs. *Dammit.* Charlie didn't need her Christmas Eve jacked with.

"Yeah, hang on." Beck pulled his phone out and started tapping the screen. "There's um...bottom drawer in that thing in the mudroom...candles, flashlights."

"Sounds good. We'll have an adventure." He went rummaging in the drawer, finding all the candles, plus batteries and a flashlight.

"Papa, where is the TV?"

"The lights are out, so we'll have to sing and snuggle. It'll be fun."

Beck sighed. "Looks like it's the whole area, Sky. No ETA yet."

Charlie followed on his heels. "What's ETA?"

That was actually a bit of a comfort, really. If it was just their house, it would be easy for the power company to blow them off until the twenty-sixth. "The whole area means sooner than later, love. ETA means when it'll get fixed. Want to run upstairs and grab some books to read?"

"TV is broken, Noah," Charlie told her brother. "I'll get books, okay?" She took a few steps and stopped. "Santa can come if the lights are out, right?"

"Santa makes his own light, sweetie. Don't you worry. He has Rudolph!"

She lit up, smiling happily. "Oh, yeah! Rudolph!"

"Great save, baby." He leaned against Beck for a second. "Lord have mercy."

"Never a dull moment. A blackout with a three-day-old baby? On Christmas Eve? Only us." Beck looked a little tired. "She's warm as anything tucked in here, though. We'll be okay. If it lasts longer than tomorrow, we'll go stay somewhere."

"Yeah. And we can charge phones in the car, if we have to. It's warm and comfy out here. We can cuddle with our family." Pizza was coming, the stove and oven worked, so they could even have coffee.

"I got books!" Charlie came back with a stack, including *How the Grinch Stole Christmas*, and set them down near the couch.

"In a little while, Charlie, you and I can take flashlights and go find the sleeping bags in the basement."

"Okay. Papa can stay with Bubba and the baby."

"I will so do that, Charlie." He winked at her.

"I can bring up some extra wood if you take the sleepy dragon from me. Or we can wait an hour or so until feeding time." Beck took a book from Charlie's stack and handed it to Noah to play with. Mostly Noah chewed on them, but sometimes he'd pretend to read.

"We can wait for feeding. We'll have to heat up cocoa too."

Charlie sat a book in his lap. "Read, Papa."

Beck chuckled. "I'll just chew on this one with Noah."

"Right on." Sky settled her against him and started with the Grinch, doing all the voices and making her giggle madly. By the end, even Noah was listening, all into the story.

Beck applauded as he said, "The end."

"Wow, Papa. You're good at that." Beck smiled at him, and there was a neat sort of wonder in his husband's eyes.

He winked. How many times had he had to tell stories to

reporters, to sponsors, to VIPs? Talking was what Sky did, when he wasn't riding.

"I like Cindy Lou's voice best. It's so funny!" Who needed electricity? Charlotte's laugh lit up the living room.

He chuckled and snuggled her in, doing his best Cindy-Lou-Who as he sang Jingle Bells.

Beck got to his feet and grabbed the box of candy canes. "These are technically for the tree, but didn't Cindy Lou have a big one in the TV show?" Beck pulled one out and opened it, then handed it to Charlie.

"Ooh. Thank you, Pappy! A candy can!"

"I need a candy can too, Pappy!" Sky grinned at Beck, waggling his eyebrows. "I like them so much. I like to suck them until they disappear."

Beck's eyebrow climbed slowly toward his hairline and he got a heated grin. "Maybe later, if Santa thinks you've been a good boy."

"Man, okay. I promise to be good." He felt wicked as all get out, and happy, all the way to the bone.

"Papa is a good boy. He reads books and makes lunch and takes care of us," Charlie insisted.

"You're right, girlie. Papa is the best." Beck laughed and tossed him a candy cane. "Oh, look who is awake." Beck sat on the couch and popped Sierra out of her sling. "Hey, baby girl."

She turned her head, searching for food, Sky was sure.

"She's a hoot. She has a hollow leg like her bubba."

Beck teased her with a finger, and she latched right on to it. "Look at her. You want to take her? I'll get a bottle."

"I would. Come here, Dragon Baby. We'll have a snuggle." She was solid and warm in his hands, and he cuddled her against his chest. "You want to hang here or help Pappy make a bottle, Charlie?"

"I go Pappy!" Noah cried. "Me!"

"You want to help, Bubba? Okay, then. Noah's turn." Beck lifted Noah up and held him flat. "We can fly to the kitchen! Zoom!"

"Zoom!" Noah repeated, giggling as they disappeared into the kitchen.

"Can I hold her?"

"Sure. Come sit in my lap and I'll hold you, and you can hold her."

"She's very little. We hafta be careful with her baby head."

"Yes. Her neck isn't strong yet. I trust you. You'll be easy."

"She has big eyes." Sierra wiggled and reached up, grabbing a fistful of Charlie's hair. "Hey!"

"Easy, baby." He got Charlie loose, prying the grasping fingers open and giving Sierra his pinky to clamp on to. "She can't control her hands and arms yet. She can't even hardly focus. She isn't trying to hurt, right?"

Charlie looked at him suspiciously. "I guess not." She looked back at Sierra. "She can't see me yet?"

"Not clear. She can see, but not focus, like...when you have sleep in your eyes and everything's fuzzy?"

Charlie nodded, watching Sierra closely. "And she doesn't understand me yet either. Pappy said so. He said we have to teach her."

Speaking of Pappy, he could hear Beck singing to Noah in the kitchen.

"Oh, yes. You're going to be the most important person in the world to her. Helping her, being the big sister, being her hero—it's a big job. I'm so glad she has you." He knew that Charlie took her job seriously already, and he prayed that it would seal her knowledge that her place in their family was unshakable.

"She's important. We have to take care of her. She can't do things for herself. Like Bubba kind of, only more."

"Right. You've taught your bubba so much. Now you have two little ones to be a big sister to. I'm so proud of you."

Noah came out of the kitchen, walking slowly with Sierra's bottle in his hands and Beck right behind him. "Are you going to feed her, Charlie?"

"Uh-huh. I'm the big sister." She glanced at him, then at Noah. "Good job, Bubba!"

God love her, that was so friggin' cute.

Noah looked ridiculously pleased with himself, grinning wide as Beck lifted him up so he could hand off the bottle. "Warm. No hot. Warm, Sister."

"Warm. That's right. Warm for the dragon sister." Beck set Noah down in his little pen again with a sippy cup of his own. "Yay for backup batteries in the bottle warmer. I panicked for a second."

"Oh, rock on. Yay." He helped Charlie get Sierra latched on, and their hungry girl sucked away.

"Okay." Beck rubbed his hands together. "I'm going to... um. Wood, sleeping bags...close some doors to keep the heat in here. You good?"

"We're just fine, Pappy. No worries. How about we go put on our fuzzy jammies after we feed Sierra? Then we can bring down our blankets and pillows and all snuggle together."

"I wonder if there's an update." Beck wandered off to the mudroom looking at his phone. "Nope!" When he appeared again, he had on snow gear. "I'll be back in a bit. Maybe we can find an M.O.V.I.E. on my iPad."

"Sounds good. We'll feed and change her and make a blanket fort. New Christmas tradition!" Lord have mercy. Santa, let the lights come on by tomorrow morning.

Beck leaned over, bracing an arm on the wall above the couch, and kissed him. "I love you. This is the best Christmas ever."

"It so is." Lights or no. They had their babies—all three of them—at home, whole and healthy.

19

Beck loaded up the wood stove and brought in lots of extra wood so it would be dry and ready to use all night. He'd found sleeping bags in the basement, and Sky brought down blankets and pillows and they'd made a toasty little nest on the family room floor.

Charlie and Noah were sound asleep, and Sky was feeding Sierra again. Maybe it was a blood thing, maybe it was a cowboy thing...he didn't know why, but she just ate better for Sky. So they had an overnight agreement that Sky did the feeding, and he did the burping and changing.

But right now, while Sky was feeding, he was playing Santa and hauling wrapped presents out of their snazzy new man cave, where they'd hidden them. They'd promised Santa would come, and lights or no lights, their kids would wake up to presents under the tree.

Jesus, the basement had really gotten cold. He'd put on his toasty slippers, his robe, and a hat, but he still found himself jogging down the stairs to keep warm.

A blackout was not the end of the world. It was another

little twist in their plans, but Sky was right; they had each other, and the rest of it would be what it would be. It would be memorable for sure.

He brought the last load up and set it quietly near the tree. He knew Sky wanted to help, so he left them in a pile so that Sky could arrange them. He almost grabbed a slice of leftover pizza but thought better of it—tomorrow, hopefully, would be a big food day. Charlie and Noah were both deep sleepers, so he wasn't too worried about waking them up as he sat next to Sky. "Hey," he whispered, sliding in close to Sky to steal some body heat. "I think I got everything."

"Good deal. Come here, babe—you're like ice." Sky drew him closer. "She's hungry, but she's nice and warm in her cocoon."

"It's cold out there. You'd think the heat was out or something." He pulled the edge of the sling out so he could get a look at the baby. "She's so beautiful. I'm so proud to be her dad." His heart was full. Every time he looked at Sierra he could hardly hold back the tears.

"We're so lucky. I was so fucking scared when I found out about Charlie and Noah. I didn't know that I could love them with my whole heart. I was wrong."

Sky had the biggest heart of anyone he'd ever met, so his husband's words seemed so strange to him. But they weren't; his worries were valid and real, and Beck understood completely. "I wasn't sure I'd ever be able to think of them as mine. I thought I'd always be living in Connor's shadow, you know? I was wrong too. These kids are ours, all of them."

"And so fast. I just...I guess this is how it's meant to be. I know I've said, but thank you for giving this to me."

Some day he would make Sky believe—really believe—

that he deserved all the good things that came his way. "Baby, I didn't give this to you. We built this together. Just like we've done with everything else that matters. Everything good that we have. This is ours. But thank you for doing it with me."

"There's no one else I'd want to make a family with." Sky stroked Sierra's cheek, their little girl blinking at him. "I wanted to be a father with you."

He remembered the night of his second proposal when Sky had first mentioned adoption. That had gotten the conversation started. He wondered how long it had been on Sky's mind before he'd finally asked. "It's funny, because I'd tried not to think about it too hard, in case you weren't interested. I didn't want to be disappointed. You really don't know how relieved I was when you finally brought it up. Surprised, but relieved to at least be having the conversation."

And look at them now. Zero to three in as many months.

"Sometimes it's hard to know what to say, how to ask for things. We're getting better at that." Sky handed Sierra over to him to burp. "I love you, babe."

As Sky said the words, the electricity came on, the lights on the tree twinkling and sparkling.

Beckett gasped. "*Oh.*" It was so beautiful—both the timing and the way their tree cast warmth in the room. He leaned in for the kiss that an amazing moment like that called for. "I love you too. Merry Christmas."

"Merry Christmas, love." Sky leaned back, eyelids going heavy. "I can't wait for them to see Santa has come."

He was looking forward to it too. For the kids. And he was looking forward to watching Sky help the kids open the presents. It was like a first Christmas for all of them.

Sierra was resting quietly, and he needed to change her, but not yet. He wanted to enjoy the tree. To see his lover sleeping under it. He took Sky's hand. "I know. It's going to be perfect." It already was.

EPILOGUE

"Papa! Papa, is Grampa coming?" Charlie was so excited she couldn't sit still.

Sky looked up from where he was fixing chili. "He's driving Granny up. They should be here any minute. They're going to stay here a week until their stuff comes for their new house."

"House!" Noah said, and Sky nodded.

"You know it, Bubba. They found a condo right in town. You'll be able to see them lots."

Beckett was changing the poopmonster, who'd blown out another diaper. Baby shit was something else.

"Grampa coming!" The boy did love his grandfather.

"Can I put more candy cans on the tree for Grampa? I bet he likes them."

"Put enough for Granny too." He handed over their last box of yumminess.

Sky stirred the hot cocoa in the Crock-pot, then checked to make sure the kitchen was as clean as their kitchen could be.

"Did I do my math right? Is she two weeks today?" Beck

came in with Sierra. She still seemed tiny in Beck's arms, but two weeks of eating had made her a pretty solid little thing. "I think that's right."

"She is. Our dragon baby." He leaned in to take a kiss.

"Rawr!" Noah was getting good at that.

"Mmm. Rawr." Beck gave him a leering grin and kissed him. "I put her in the little jumper Mom sent. I thought that would go over well."

"She'll be excited. I toned down the chili for stomachs old and young. I think it'll—"

"They're *here*!" Charlie's squeal set Bruiser to barking, and Walter climbed his cat tree, hissing.

"Oh, Walter. Don't be so antisocial." Beck looked at him and grinned. "Just save some heat for me, cowboy."

The car horn honked, which was just exactly what Bruiser needed.

Charlie bounced at the door, Bruiser howled, Sierra started screaming, and Noah threw a handful of Cheerios in the air like confetti.

Excellent.

"Charlie, open the door, sweetie! Let Bruiser out before he busts something." Beck started bouncing Sierra. "Mom is here. She'll have this under control in sixteen seconds."

Charlie opened the door and Bruiser shot out, knocking her over. But his little cowgirl didn't cry; she got right up and shouted, "Dammit, Bruiser!"

She sounded just like Beck.

"Shit." Beck snorted a laugh.

"I'm so getting your happy ass a swear jar." He stopped Noah from throwing more cereal and scooped his son up. "Come see Granny and Grampa. They're here! Yay!"

"Yay!" Noah echoed and let Sky set him on his feet.

Mom appeared a second later, holding Charlie's hand.

"Your father is out there with Bruiser. He's been talking about getting a dog for weeks now." She went to Sky and kissed his cheek. "Hello, Skyler."

"Hey, Mom. I think Charlie has someone to introduce you to. Right Charlie-girl?" He watched Charlie take her over to Sierra.

"Granny, this is my little sister. The dragon baby."

Beck showed her off, and as soon as Mom smiled, Beck beamed like the proud father he was. "Isn't she gorgeous, Mom? You want to hold her? She's a little fussy but—"

"I know all about fussy. Your sister had croup all the time." Mom took Sierra easily. "Charlie, let's go sit. Will you sit with me and Sierra?"

"Uh-huh." And just like that, Mom had the baby and Charlie quiet.

"Baby, Noah's eating Cheerios off the floor." Beck pointed.

"I mopped yesterday." A little dirt wouldn't hurt him, right?

Beck shrugged and winked. "Oh. Okay, then."

"Hello? Where's my Noah?" Dad came in, deep voice filling the front hall.

"Gampa!" Noah ran to Dad, who scooped him up. Bruiser shook off and headed for his bed by the wood stove.

"Hey, Dad." Beck gave him a quick hug. "How was the drive?"

"Fine. Long, but the stops along the way were good. Mom doesn't like those roadside hotels much, but she did fine."

"Well, y'all can have a nice room here. It's all shiny and new." Sky nodded to Beck's dad and grinned. "Someone there has been so ready for you to come."

Dad smiled. "I missed this little face. Both of them. Noah. Where is your new sister?"

Noah pointed. "Sister!"

"Well, let's go see. My goodness, she is pretty tiny, huh?"

Mom smiled at Dad. "Doesn't she have the sweetest little cheeks?"

Beck looked around, this way and that, like he'd lost something, then grinned at Sky. "Wait. I'm not holding a kid. Are you holding a kid?"

Sky looked at his arms, going wide-eyed as he gasped dramatically. He could so play along with this game. Beck had learned to play again, and it was magical. "I appear to be kidless. What happened?"

"I don't know. Those people took them, and they all look so happy, don't they? It's amazing. And there's finally some room in my arms for you, handsome husband." Beck caught him with one arm and pulled him in. "How about that?"

Skyler leaned hard, watching as Beckett's parents listened and loved and oohed and aahed. It made him tickled as anything. He lifted his face for a kiss while no one was watching.

Beck bent and gave him his kiss; one that felt a little like hello, a little like I love you, and a lot like maybe it might be a hot tub night.

Whatever was coming, Sky was in, balls to bones.

He was ready.

JUST DEX
Book One in the Les's Bar Series
By Jodi Payne and BA Tortuga

When Dexter Appleton's best friend Huck commits suicide, it damn near kills Dex too. Huck was a bull rider with a crazy life, and leaves behind a big house, and a ton of unanswered questions. But Dex is just a simple guy, just a Texas redneck trying to scrape together a life, and he can't handle much more before he breaks.

Cyrus Hughes is a professional Dom. He's shocked to learn that Huck is gone, he's met with Huck twice a month for years, and didn't expected to miss a client so much. When he heads to Texas to pay his respects, he instinctively feels protective of Huck's anxious and unlikely best friend, Dexter.

The attraction between them grows, even long distance, until Cyrus insists he needs Dex with him in New York. Clinging to his last bit of hope, Dex takes a leap of faith and moves what little he still owns in with Cyrus, hoping to find his place is in the world, and learn how to love a lifestyle Dom.

Their path is full of trial and error, adjusting expectations and discovering how they fit together. Cyrus and Dex try to smooth out the rough edges and create their own family, one where Cyrus hopes to convince Dex that he's not "just" anything.

COMING JANUARY 2021

ABOUT JODI

JODI takes herself way too seriously and has been known to randomly break out in song. Her men are imperfect but genuine, stubborn but likable, often kinky, and frequently their own worst enemies. They are characters you can't help but fall in love with while they stumble along the path to their happily ever after. For those looking to get on her good side, Jodi's addictions include nonfat lattes, Malbec and tequila any way you pour it.

Website: jodipayne.net

Newsletter: http://bit.ly/whatsupjodi

All Jodi's Social Links: linktr.ee/jodipayne

ABOUT BA

Texan to the bone and an unrepentant Daddy's Girl, BA Tortuga spends her days with her basset hounds, getting tattooed, texting her grandbabies, and eating Mexican food. When she's not doing that, she's writing. She spends her days off watching rodeo, knitting and surfing Pinterest in the name of research. BA's personal saviors include her wife, Julia Talbot, her best friends, and coffee. Lots of coffee. Really good coffee.

Having written everything from fist-fighting rednecks to hard-core cowboys to werewolves, BA does her damnedest to tell the stories of her heart, which was raised in Northeast Texas, but has heard the call of the high desert and lives in the Sandias. With books ranging from hard-hitting GLBT romance, to fiery ménages, to the most traditional of love stories, BA refuses to be pigeon-holed by anyone but the voices in her head.

BA loves to talk to her readers and can be found at http:// batortuga.com/ and her newsletter signup link is http:// bit.ly/BAJulianews

AVAILABLE FROM JODI & BA

The Collaborations Series

Refraction

Syncopation

East Meets Westerns

(single titles)

Heart of a Redneck

Wrecked

Land of Enchantment

Window Dressing

Flying Blind

Special Delivery, A Wrecked Holiday Novel

The Cowboy and the Dom Trilogy

First Rodeo, Book One

Razor's Edge, Book Two

No Ghosts, Book Three

The Soldier and the Angel

The Triskelion Series

Breaking the Rules

Interested in learning more about BA's cowboys and Jodi's gentlemen? Want free fiction and news? Join our newsletters!

What's Up with Jodi
http://bit.ly/whatsupjodi

Spurs and Shifters
https://lp.constantcontact.com/su/A9CRUzp/baandjulia